WHAT'S GONE

(A Peyton Risk Suspense Thriller —Book 4)

Ella Swift

Ella Swift

Ella Swift is author of the PEYTON RISK mystery series, comprising five books (and counting).

An avid reader and lifelong fan of the mystery and thriller genres, Ella loves to hear from you, so please feel free to visit ellaswiftauthor.com to learn more and stay in touch.

BOOKS BY ELLA SWIFT

PEYTON RISK MYSTERY SERIES
WHAT'S HIS (Book #1)
WHAT'S LEFT (Book #2)
WHAT'S WISHED (Book #3)
WHAT'S GONE (Book #4)
WHAT'S MINE (Book #5)

PROLOGUE

Jennifer Easton's eyelids fluttered open, her vision blurred and unfocused. The sky above her was a jigsaw puzzle of clouds, their edges tinged with the fading hues of sunset. She blinked rapidly—she had to clear her mind and make sense of the situation. The damp air clung to her like a second skin, and she shivered as cold water sloshed against her body.

"Where am I?" she muttered under her breath, her voice strained from disuse.

As her eyes adjusted, Jennifer took in the small boat surrounding her. It was a rickety thing, barely big enough for her to stretch out in. The wooden planks that formed its hull were weathered and covered in a layer of green algae, testament to the many years it had spent in the murky waters of the swamp. A sour odor filled the air, a mix of stagnant water and decaying vegetation.

Pushing herself up on shaky arms, Jennifer attempted to sit upright, but an unexpected constriction around her neck stopped her short. She clawed at the offending object, her fingers finding a thick vine wrapped tightly around her throat.

"Get off!" she gasped, her heart pounding in her ears as panic set in.

She struggled with the unyielding vine, her nails digging into its fibrous surface, but it refused to budge. The more she pulled, the tighter it seemed to become, threatening to choke the life from her.

Jennifer coughed hoarsely, the pressure against her windpipe increasing with each futile tug. It was as if the vine had a life of its own, tightening around her neck like a ruthless predator. Suddenly, she stopped struggling, the reality of her plight sinking in.

"Help!" she screamed, hoping someone would hear her desperate plea.

Sensing the tautness of the vine, she scooted backward to release the pressure. She was facing the stern of the boat, being towed through the murky waters of a swamp—she was in Louisiana, she remembered that much. But how? What was pulling her?

Turning around, she spotted an airboat only a short distance away, its flat-bottomed hull and large caged fan distinctly visible as it cut

1

through the algae-covered water. The droning hum of its motor filled the air, drowning out all other sounds.

This can't be happening, Jennifer thought.

Jennifer glanced down at the vine tightening around her neck, then followed its trail to the airboat. The thick green tendril was wrapped several times around one of the boat's metal struts, secured in place not only by its own strength but also by a series of knots.

"Hey!" Jennifer screamed, her voice hoarse from strain and fear. "Help me!"

Her cries seemed to fall on deaf ears as the figure piloting the airboat remained unmoved. He stood tall, his broad shoulders hunched slightly forward as he gripped the steering stick. A wide-brimmed hat obscured most of his features, but from what little she could see, his clothing appeared functional and rugged—the attire of someone who knew the swamps intimately.

"Please, I'm begging you!" Jennifer's voice cracked, her desperation mounting. "I don't know what's going on, but I need your help!"

Her mind raced backward, searching for any clue as to how she'd ended up in this perilous situation. Earlier that day, she had been conducting research for her marketing consultancy firm, exploring the swamps of Louisiana for untapped tourism opportunities. The vibrant landscapes were a far cry from the concrete jungle of New York City she called home, and she had been eager to uncover their secrets.

She remembered meeting with some locals at a bar on the outskirts of town. They had been hesitant to share their knowledge about the swamp, eyeing her expensive suit and polished shoes with suspicion. So she'd started drinking with them, hoping it would loosen them up.

And then...

Well, that was about where the memory ended, wasn't it? The next thing was waking here, in this boat.

"Damn it, Jennifer," she muttered to herself, her hands shaking as she grasped the vine wrapped around her neck. She couldn't believe how foolish she had been to drink so much with the locals. At twenty-eight, she was far from being a naive teenager, but in her eagerness to fit in, she had let her guard down.

I have to get out of here, she thought. *Whoever that man is, he's certainly not my friend.*

"Help!" she screamed, hoping someone might hear her above the din of the airboat engine. Glancing over, she saw the figure in the airboat turn slowly to face her. The man's face was obscured by the shadow cast by his wide-brimmed hat, making it impossible for Jennifer to discern his features.

"What do you want?" she cried. "Is it money? I can get you money!"

The man remained silent, his gaze fixed on her as if he were studying a specimen trapped in a web. Jennifer's chest tightened with fear, and she redoubled her efforts to free herself from the vine's grasp.

"Please," she begged again, tears streaming down her cheeks as she clawed at the unyielding fibers. "I'll give you anything. Just help me!"

But the stranger only stood there, his silence more terrifying than any threat he could have uttered. It was then that Jennifer knew, deep in her bones, that this man would not be her savior. If she was going to survive, she would have to save herself.

The man's movements were deliberate and unhurried as he drew a gleaming knife from his belt. Jennifer watched, confused and uneasy, as he set the blade against the rope that tethered the two boats together. The metal bit into the fibers, severing them with slow precision. Panic welled up in Jennifer's chest as she finally understood what was happening.

"Wait! Stop!" she screamed, her voice raw with desperation. "Please, don't do this!"

The man continued to saw through the rope, ignoring her pleas as if they were nothing more than the hum of the airboat engine. She couldn't see his eyes beneath the brim of his hat, but she knew he could hear her. He didn't care. He wanted her to suffer, and there was nothing she could offer to change his mind.

"Please!" she cried again, but he gave no response. As the rope frayed under his relentless assault, Jennifer felt a sinking dread in the pit of her stomach.

As soon as that rope breaks, the only thing holding our boats together will be the vine around my neck. She could grab hold of the vine, try to take some of the pressure off her throat...but for how long? How long before her fingers slipped, her strength gave out, and she was dragged down into the murky depths of the swamp? The image of herself choking, gasping for air that wouldn't come, filled her mind, fueling her desperation to escape.

She was running out of options; she needed to come up with a plan, fast.

Don't panic, she thought, gripping the sides of the small boat. *Think. What can you do? There has to be something.*

Maybe, if she pulled hard enough, she could snap the vine. It was worth a try.

Bracing herself, she wrapped her fingers tightly around the vine. She pulled, her muscles screaming in protest, but the vine held firm. Its coarse texture bit into her sweaty hands, drawing pinpricks of blood.

"Damn it," she hissed through gritted teeth, switching her focus to the knot. If she couldn't break the vine, maybe she could untie it? Her trembling fingers fumbled with the knot, but it was as solid and unyielding as a rock.

Desperate and out of ideas, she glanced wildly around the boat. Amongst a pile of grimy ropes and rusted tools, her eyes landed on an old pair of pliers in the bottom of the boat. If she could just reach it...

Realizing there was no way her hand would be able to reach the pliers, she decided to lean back and use her foot instead. She was wearing sneakers, the white around the edge darkened to a dull brown by dried swamp mud and grime. Heart pounding, she stretched her leg slowly toward the tool. She could feel the vine tightening as she strained, sending sparks of pain through her neck.

She cried out as the vine bit deeper into her flesh, but she was close, so close, just a few centimeters away from the pliers. Once she had the pliers in hand, all she would have to do is saw at the vine with the pliers' sharp edge. She was so close to escape, so close to freedom.

She managed to nudge the pliers toward herself. Then, nearly frantic with excitement now, she stepped on the pliers and slid them closer. All she had to do now was reach out and—

Just then, as Jennifer was leaning forward, the airboat's motor started up. The rope tethering the two boats together must have already snapped, because as soon as the airboat moved, Jennifer felt herself pulled back against the bow of the boat, the plier now several feet out of reach.

She clung to the edges of the boat to keep from being pulled into the water. But she could not resist the pressure around her throat—it would snap her neck if she resisted it any longer. As the darkness filled her vision, she felt herself letting go and plunging over the bow of the boat.

Down into the churning, murky depths of the swamp.

CHAPTER ONE

Peyton Risk's slender fingers combed through the filing cabinet, flipping through tax documents one by one and tossing them aside with a frustrated sigh.

It's got to be here somewhere, she thought.

The storage shed in which she stood was filled to the brim with furniture and other items that had once belonged to her parents, relics of a happier time. Dust particles danced in the dim, early morning light that filtered through the open door, casting hazy shadows upon the worn-out couch, the old easel where her mother had painted, and the workbench her father used for his carpentry projects.

Sixteen years ago, Peyton's parents had been mysteriously killed in Eden's Gate National Park. The pain of their loss still lingered in Peyton's heart like a stubborn splinter, refusing to be dislodged. It wasn't until recently that she had decided to reopen the investigation, fueled by a restless desire for closure and justice.

During her search for answers, Peyton had come across a recording her father, Galen, sent to a ranger before his death. In the audio, Galen mentioned a place called Red Pine Cabin in Sprucewood Park—a location Peyton had never heard of before. Determined to find this elusive cabin, she was now delving into her parents' belongings, hoping to uncover any clues about its whereabouts.

"Where could it be?" she muttered under her breath, her hazel eyes scanning the endless sea of papers.

Her hand paused as she pulled out an old map, creased and yellowed with age. She unfolded it carefully, revealing a detailed layout of Sprucewood Park. Peyton's heart raced with anticipation as she studied the map, her fingers tracing the winding trails and landmarks.

"Come on, Red Pine Cabin...where are you?" she whispered. She leaned in closer, her dark chestnut hair falling over her shoulders like a curtain.

Nothing about the map, however, suggested the location of Red Pine Cabin. It was just a park map—one of dozens, maybe hundreds, her parents had owned.

Peyton tossed the map aside and sighed, rubbing her temples as she leaned against the cold metal filing cabinet. The storage shed was a mess of papers and boxes, evidence of her tireless search for information about the elusive Red Pine Cabin. For seven days now, she had been combing through every document, every scrap of paper, trying to find even the slightest clue that would lead her to the cabin's location.

She had only been going at it for a few hours this morning, but already her eyes were tired, and her muscles ached from the hours she'd spent moving furniture around in the cluttered space over the past week. But she knew she couldn't stop now, not when her parents' murders remained unsolved. She owed it to them to see this through—to find the truth behind their tragic deaths.

"Maybe...maybe the cabin has nothing to do with their murders," she murmured, doubt creeping into her voice. She pressed her fingers to her forehead, trying to ward off the headache that threatened to consume her.

Just then, Peyton heard the scuff of a footstep. She looked up, startled, and found herself staring at Owen Banks, the owner of Mountain View Storage.

"Hey, Peyton. You alright?" he asked, genuine concern in his eyes.

Owen was a tall man with short-cropped sandy hair and a perpetual five o'clock shadow. His sharp features were softened by kind blue eyes that always seemed to be studying the world around him. He wore a simple plaid shirt and jeans, a far cry from the tailored suits he used to wear during their time at the FBI together. Back then, Owen had been an analyst while Peyton worked as a field agent, and they'd formed a bond built on mutual respect and trust.

"Hi, Owen," she said, trying to smile despite her exhaustion. "Yeah, I'm fine. Just going through some of my parents' things."

Peyton was grateful for the generosity Owen had shown her, allowing her to use this storage unit free of charge while she renovated her family's cabin. In a way, it felt like he was helping her piece together the fragments of her past—a task that had proven to be both challenging and emotionally draining.

"You didn't sleep here last night, did you?" Owen asked, sounding worried as he glanced around the cluttered unit.

"No, of course not," Peyton said. *I slept in my car,* she added mentally. *If it can be called sleep.*

"Well, whatever the case, I really think you could use a break."

Peyton sighed. "I wish I could. It's just that I feel like the answer is here somewhere. If I can find any information about this Red Pine Cabin my dad mentioned, it could finally give me the closure I need."

She slumped down on the worn couch, releasing the tension that had built up in her shoulders over the past several days. Owen sat down beside her, his eyes filled with understanding.

"I know how important this is to you," he said gently. "But you also need to take care of yourself. When's the last time you had a decent meal or a good night's sleep?"

Peyton gave a weary smile. "It's been a while," she admitted.

Owen was right—in her relentless pursuit of the truth, she had neglected to take care of herself. The long hours hunched over documents and maps had taken their toll, both mentally and physically.

"Why don't you let me make you some breakfast?" Owen suggested. "My cabin's just down the road. Get away from all this for a bit." He gestured around the cluttered storage unit.

Peyton shook her head. "I really should keep going. Don't want to lose my momentum."

"I have to run some errands, so I can't do lunch, but how about dinner? My treat."

Peyton hesitated, biting her lip. As much as Owen's invitation appealed to her, the thought of stepping away, even for an evening, filled her with guilt. What if the answer was right here, buried somewhere in this mess of papers?

Yet she was exhausted, both mentally and physically. She could push herself a little while longer, but if she didn't take a break soon, she'd be in no shape to continue her search.

Peyton nodded slowly, realizing Owen was right. "Alright, you've convinced me," she said, managing a tired smile. "I could really use a home-cooked meal."

Owen grinned and clapped a hand on her shoulder. "Atta girl. I'll see you for dinner, then. You know the way, right?"

"I've seen it, yeah."

"Excellent. I'll throw some steaks on the grill—should have everything ready around, say, six? You're welcome earlier, though. I should be at the house from about two o'clock on."

Peyton smiled. "Thanks, Owen."

As Owen left, Peyton looked around the storage room once more. Spotting her father's old desk chair, she sank down into it, letting its familiar creaks envelop her. The chair listed slightly to the side, so she leaned the other way to compensate.

I just need a moment to rest my eyes, she told herself. *Just a moment to pull myself together.*

As exhausted as she was from the emotional turmoil of the week, it didn't take her long to fall asleep, and soon she was wrapped up in a strange dream.

In her dream, she was back in Eden's Gate National Park with her parents, a memory tinged with the surreal hues of dreamscape. The sun hung low in the sky, casting a golden glow over the forest as her father strung up their food from the trees in a hanging bear cache.

"But won't the bear see it?" she asked. "Shouldn't we hide it?"

"You can't hide food from a bear's nose," her father said, tapping the bridge of his own nose. "Besides, it doesn't matter if the bear can see the food so long as he can't reach it. If you want to stop a bear, you have to think like one."

Peyton jerked awake, her father's words echoing in her mind. She blinked in the dim light of the storage unit, disoriented. How long had she been asleep? The dream had felt so vivid, so real.

She checked her phone. She'd been asleep for three hours. She wasn't yet late for dinner with Owen, so that was something. As she rose and headed for the door, however, she thought about her father's words in the dream.

Think like a bear, she mused.

It occurred to her that, in searching this storage unit, she had followed a process very different from the one she'd have used as an investigator. But what if she treated her dad like a suspect and this storage unit like it was a crime scene? How might she search it differently?

"Approach this like you're on the trail of a suspect," Peyton murmured to herself, channeling her years of experience with the FBI. "Look for anomalies, patterns, and connections."

As she surveyed the room once more, Peyton's gaze fell on the armchair. *Why doesn't it sit right?* she wondered. It was possible something had happened to one of the legs...but then again, her father had been a carpenter. If his chair had been broken, he would've fixed it.

Peyton grabbed the chair and tipped it back, exposing the wooden legs. One of the legs – the one that caused the chair to list to the side – was missing the foot, and there was a hollow space inside the leg that the foot had fit into.

Holding her breath, Peyton reached into this hollow space and felt around. She felt something smooth—tape? She dug at it, peeling the tape back and exposing something small and plastic.

Whatever it is, she thought, *he must've been in a hurry to hide it. Otherwise, he would've found a way to put the foot back on.*

Peeling the tape free, Peyton managed to pull the object out. She held it up, staring at it.

It was a USB drive.

With a pounding heart, Peyton retrieved her laptop from her backpack and slid the USB drive into the port.

CHAPTER TWO

Sean O'Malley's muscles strained as he performed another pull-up on the tree branch.

Thirty-two, he thought.

He was in the middle of an intense workout, sweat dripping down his face as he pushed himself to the limit. The sun had only been up for an hour or two, and it cast a soft golden light over the small park where he preferred to train. The park, located near his home, provided a serene backdrop for his morning routine—the perfect setting for his focused mind and disciplined body.

He had already completed a five-mile run, followed by calisthenics and strength training. Growing up in Montana, Sean had learned the importance of physical fitness and its role in wilderness survival. It was a lesson that he carried into his career with the National Park Service.

As he dropped from the branch, the final pull-up complete, Sean glanced at his watch. *Time to wrap it up,* he thought, wiping the sweat from his brow. He took a moment to stretch out his muscles, feeling the satisfying burn of a hard-earned workout. Satisfied, he jogged back to his house to clean up and prepare for the day ahead.

Just then, as he was jogging, he felt his phone buzz. He stopped to lean against a tree and pulled his phone out, noting several unread text messages from Peter Marshal, his boss and the head of the NPS. It looked like Sean had been assigned to a new case, a series of murders in Louisiana. The last message read, *Any idea where Peyton is??? can't reach her*

I'll find her, Sean wrote back.

Sean's relationship with Peyton Risk had started off rocky, but over time, they had formed a solid partnership. She was dedicated and passionate about her work—traits he admired and respected. She was full of surprises, and he had to admit that, despite his initial reservations, they made a formidable team.

Sean dialed Peyton's number and waited.

"Come on, Peyton," he muttered under his breath, frustration mounting as the call went to voicemail. He tried again, but still, no answer.

Suddenly, he felt a sense of urgency rising. Sean was not one to worry unduly, but their line of work carried risks, and Peyton was not one to shirk duty. Was it possible she was in trouble?

As Sean resumed his jog, he thought back to the last time he'd spoken with Peyton a few days ago to tidy up some details about their last investigation. She'd said something about going through her parents' things—but where had she been? At her parents' cabin?

No, he thought, *not her cabin. It sounded like the items were in storage. But where?*

He tried to remember, but he didn't think she'd mentioned the name of the place. So how was he to reach her?

As he made his way through the park, passing several joggers coming the opposite direction, he thought about Dale Everhart, a friend of his from the NSA. If anyone could track a phone to find the user's location, it was Dale.

Besides, Dale owed him a favor.

Sean pulled out his phone again and dialed Dale's number. The phone rang once, twice, before a groggy voice picked up on the other end.

"Everhart." It sounded like Dale had been in a deep slumber.

"Dale, it's O'Malley. I need a favor."

"What time is it, O'Malley?" Dale yawned audibly over the phone. Then he cursed. "It's four in the morning, man."

"Seven."

"Four my time."

Sean winced. He was still in D.C. where he'd had a meeting with his boss the night before, just a routine set of questions about his last report, but Dale was all the way out in Washington—three hours behind Sean.

"Never mind that," Sean said, "I need you to pull up some coordinates."

There was a pause from Dale's end as he presumably processed this unusual request in his half-awake state. "Can't this wait till later?"

"No, it can't."

"Does this mean you're calling in that favor?"

A few years earlier, Sean had helped Dale by diverting a potential PR disaster involving an NSA employee who had recklessly endangered a National Park. That favor had been stored away, unspent until now.

"Yes," Sean affirmed. "I'm calling it in."

"Alright, alright." Dale's voice was filled with resignation. "Give me a minute."

Sean stayed on the line, his gaze drifting across the park as the sun began to rise higher in the sky. A few yards away, a squirrel scampered up a tree trunk, its bushy tail twitching excitedly. He watched it for a moment before pulling his attention back to the task at hand.

Eventually, Dale came back on the line. "Okay, shoot."

Sean gave him Peyton's number and resumed his jog while Dale did whatever it was NSA analysts did to track down someone's coordinates.

"So," Dale asked as he typed away on a keyboard, "is she cute?"

"Is who cute?" Sean asked, puzzled.

"This Peyton Risk. You know what? I can just look up a picture myself." There was a pause, followed by a low whistle. "Not bad, Sean. Although I have to say this stalking business worries me a bit. You could just ask her out."

"We're not dating," Sean said.

"Why not? She's pretty."

"She's also my partner, and I need to find her. She's not answering her phone." It was true he found Peyton attractive, but so what? Dating a coworker could be awfully messy, and besides, he didn't have any idea whether she had the least interest in him.

"Sure, sure." There was a teasing note in Dale's voice that Sean ignored. This wasn't the time for jokes or friendly banter.

"Okay, I have her location," Dale finally said, serious now. "It looks like she has a storage facility called 'Mountain View Storage.' Heard of it?"

"No," Sean said as his car came within view. "Thanks, Dale."

"We're even-steven now, right?"

"Right. Go back to sleep, Dale."

"With pleasure."

Sean grinned as he ended the call. Then his face grew serious again. What, he wondered, was Peyton doing at a storage facility? And more importantly, why wasn't she answering her phone?

***

As Sean pulled up at Peyton's storage unit at Mountain View Storage, he noticed her sitting in an old chair, her eyes glued to a laptop screen. She seemed so engrossed in whatever she was reading that she didn't even acknowledge his arrival.

Man, she looks beat, Sean thought. Still, even with circles beneath her eyes, Sean had to admit he had an attractive partner. Those chestnut curls alone were enough to get a man thinking.

Sean got out of the truck and approached Peyton cautiously, not wanting to alarm her. "Hey, Peyton," he said softly as he drew nearer.

She glanced up at him sharply, clearly surprised. Then, she hurriedly closed the laptop and plastered a smile onto her face.

"Oh, hey, Sean. What's up? How'd you find me here?"

"Pulled some strings," Sean said, still thinking about the expression on her face when she saw him—not just surprise, but something else as well. Shame? Guilt?

"Are you okay?" he asked.

"Of course." Her smile tightened. "Why?"

Sean knew better than to take her words at face value. He had worked with Peyton long enough to read her expressions well, and it was clear that something was wrong. "Peyton, I know you," he said. "You're not fine. What's going on?"

Peyton hesitated for a moment before responding, her fingers fidgeting with the driftwood and seaglass necklace she always wore. "It's just...some information I found while researching my parents' case. It's nothing major."

"Nothing major?" Sean raised an eyebrow, concern evident in his voice. "You look like you've just seen a ghost, Peyton. If there's something bothering you about this case, we should talk about it. We're partners, remember?"

She gazed at him, and for a few seconds he thought she might open up. Then she shook her head and asked, "I'm sorry, what did you say you're doing here?"

"We have a new case," he said, pulling out his phone to show her the messages from Marshal. "Four murders in Louisiana."

Peyton glanced at the screen but didn't seem particularly focused on it. "Louisiana?" she asked absent-mindedly, her mind clearly somewhere else. Her gaze wandered back to the closed laptop.

What's going on with you? Sean wondered. He considered pressing her, but he had the impression that whatever was on her mind, it was serious. He didn't want to upset her by intruding on her privacy any more than he already had.

"What kind of murders?" Peyton asked.

"Stranglings, apparently."

"Interesting," Peyton said, but her tone was distant. She was here

13

with him physically, but mentally, she was miles away. Sean sighed. This was not like her at all.

Screw it, he thought. *I need to know what's going on.* He cleared his throat and was about to ask her once again what was on her mind, but just then a truck pulled up, and Sean and Peyton both turned to see who it was.

"Owen," Peyton said with a self-accusing facepalm. "I was going to have dinner with him—we'll have to reschedule, though. I'll handle this."

Puzzled, Sean watched as Peyton hurried out. Sean moved closer to the laptop. He could open it, see what Peyton had been looking at...

Yes, but that would be breaking her trust. Do you really want to do that?

No. No, he did not. She could tell him when she was good and ready—assuming such a time ever came. He hoped she wouldn't make him wait long.

Just as he began to turn away, however, he noticed a thumb drive sticking out the side of the laptop. The thumb drive, unlike the laptop, had cobwebs stuck to it—and tape.

Sean looked around, the gears in his mind whirring. Had Peyton found that thumb drive in here? And more importantly...what was on it?

CHAPTER THREE

The moment Peyton stepped off the plane in Louisiana, she was hit by a wave of hot, humid air. It was an oppressive heaviness that clung to her skin, a stark contrast to the crisp, cool air she'd left behind in Virginia. The air itself seemed to have weight to it, laden as it was with moisture.

"Welcome to Louisiana," muttered Sean, brushing off a mosquito that had landed on his arm. "This is going to be a far cry from our usual stomping grounds."

Peyton took a moment to study her partner. She had to admit he looked good in his tropical-print shirt and khaki shorts, a look that was uncharacteristically casual for him. The corner of her mouth twitched upward in a half-smile.

"Got to admit, I didn't expect to see you in anything other than your standard black suit," she teased, adjusting her sunglasses on her nose.

Sean chuckled, but his eyes were squinting against the unforgiving Louisiana sun. "I figured it's better to blend in when we're out here," he said, tugging at his collar uncomfortably.

Peyton scanned the small airfield, expecting to see someone waiting for them, but it was strangely empty. A sense of unease settled over her.

"Sean, wasn't someone supposed to meet us here?" she asked.

"Yeah," he replied, looking equally puzzled. "Maybe we're early?"

She checked her watch and shook her head. "No, we're right on time. So where are they?"

Sean retrieved his phone and attempted to call their contact, but there was no answer. The unease Peyton felt began to grow into concern, especially given the recent events that had brought them to Louisiana in the first place.

Just then, the sound of music caught Peyton's attention, pulling her gaze from the empty airfield to a beat-up truck barreling toward them. The vehicle appeared as if it had been through hell and back; its paint was chipped and faded, revealing patches of rust underneath. The truck's bed was filled with an assortment of tools and equipment, some precariously held together by frayed ropes.

As the truck sped closer, Peyton instinctively took a step back, her heart hammering in her chest. She glanced at Sean, who seemed equally alarmed.

"Is this guy trying to kill us?" she muttered under her breath, her eyes locked on the approaching vehicle.

Peyton's heart raced faster as the truck showed no signs of slowing down. Just when she was sure it would plow right into them, the driver slammed on the brakes, sending a cloud of dust swirling around the tires. The truck skidded to a halt mere feet away from where they stood, its engine rumbling like an angry beast.

The driver leaned out the window, a grizzled old man with a sweaty baseball cap pulled low over his weathered face. His wiry beard resembled tangled steel wool, and a lit cigarette dangled precariously between his teeth. He gave them a crooked grin, which did little to ease Peyton's anxiety.

"Y'all must be the two NPS officers I was told to pick up," he drawled, his voice thick with a Southern accent. "Hop on in."

Peyton eyed Sean, her hazel eyes searching for reassurance. "Is this the guy we're supposed to meet?" she asked in a low voice.

Sean frowned and turned toward Chip. "Are you Tolliver?"

"Ah, no," Chip replied, chuckling as he flicked ash from his cigarette out the window. "Tolliver couldn't make it. He asked me to pick y'all up instead. Name's Chip."

Peyton exchanged another glance with Sean, who gave her a shrug as if to say, *What else can we do?* Reluctantly, Peyton grabbed her bag and settled into the truck's worn passenger seat. The truck's interior was musty, reeking of stale cigarette smoke and dampness. She wrinkled her nose in distaste but said nothing, not wanting to offend their driver.

As soon as they were settled, Chip revved the engine and began driving away from the airfield. Peyton glanced down at his right hand on the steering wheel and noticed that he was missing three fingers. She couldn't help but wonder about the story behind it, but she opted not to ask, fearing it might be a sensitive topic.

"Is this something you do often?" Peyton asked instead, trying to distract herself from her unease. "Chauffeuring people around, I mean."

Chip laughed, the sound raspy and laced with years of tobacco use. "That's a fancy word! Nah, not really. But I'm a tour guide by trade, so I know all the locals around here. And I help out the rangers from time to time, since my brother-in-law, Dayton Wilder, is one of 'em."

"Ah, I see," Peyton murmured, her gaze drifting over the passing landscape. She tried to focus on Chip's words, but her attention kept drifting back to the missing fingers, the nagging curiosity refusing to let go. She clenched her fists, feeling the tension knotting in her shoulders.

"You're here about those murders, ain't you?" Chip asked, studying Peyton and Sean shrewdly in the mirror.

"What do you know about them?" Sean asked.

"Only what everyone else knows. Seems like we got ourselves a serial killer on the loose." He chuckled. "But don't worry, I'll make sure y'all are safe while you're here."

The Louisiana landscape unfurled before them like a lush, verdant tapestry. Peyton's eyes roved over the passing scenery, taking in the towering cypress trees draped in Spanish moss, their knobby roots reaching out of the earth like gnarled hands. Swamps began to dominate the view, their dark waters reflecting the dappled sunlight filtering through the dense canopy above.

"Look at that," Sean murmured, pointing out an alligator lounging on a half-submerged log not far from the road. Peyton could see the reptile's unblinking eyes, like black marbles, watching them as they drove past. The air was thick with humidity and the scent of decaying plant matter, and she could hear the cacophony of insects and bird calls filling the air like a discordant symphony.

"Been a while since I've been down this way," Chip said, steering the truck around a bend in the road. "Always loved these parts, though. Feels like you're stepping back in time, don't it?"

Peyton nodded silently, her thoughts drifting back to her parents and the many trips they had taken together exploring the wilds of America. This place was so different from the forests and mountains of Wyoming or Virginia, yet it held its own untamed beauty.

"Hold on!" Chip suddenly shouted, swerving the truck to avoid a massive water moccasin as it slithered across the roadway. Peyton instinctively grabbed the door, heart pounding in her chest as the snake vanished into the underbrush.

"Never a dull moment around here," Chip said with a chuckle. Peyton glanced over at Sean, who seemed equally unnerved by their surroundings and their current companion.

As they continued deeper into the swamp, the road narrowed until it was little more than a dirt path. Chip slowed the truck to a crawl and then abruptly pulled to a stop at the edge of an eerily still body of water.

"Uh, Chip?" Peyton asked hesitantly. "Why are we stopping?"

"Can't drive any farther," he replied, killing the engine and climbing out of the truck. "From here on, it's airboats only."

Peyton exchanged a wary glance with Sean before they too exited the vehicle. The swamp around them looked like something from a nightmare, its dark waters barely visible beneath a layer of algae and fallen leaves. Cypress trees loomed overhead like satin-clad ghosts.

"Come on, you two," Chip called. "Let's get going. We've got a long way to go, and daylight's burning."

"Sean, are we sure we can trust this guy?" Peyton whispered, unable to shake the feeling that something was off about their impromptu guide. "I mean, he just showed up out of nowhere. Who knows where he could be taking us?"

Sean frowned, his blue eyes meeting hers with a mixture of concern and determination. He pulled out his phone. "I'll give Wilder a call. He's the one we'll be working with down here."

Peyton waited as Sean made his call. Chip had wandered a short distance away, seemingly engrossed in preparing the dilapidated airboat for their journey. Its paint was faded, the once-vibrant colors now reduced to a patchwork of greens and browns that seemed to blend seamlessly with the swamp itself. The metal frame was rusted, creaking ominously as Chip shifted his weight on the narrow deck.

"Hello, Officer Wilder," Sean said into the phone. "This is Ranger Sean O'Malley. My partner and I..." He paused. "Yes, that's correct. It was my understanding we were going to be picked up by someone by the name of John Tolliver, but instead... Uh-huh. Yes, he's here..."

Peyton watched Sean's face closely as he spoke, analyzing each subtle change in his expression. He seemed relieved, which eased her tension a little.

Sean sighed. "I understand. Thank you for clarifying that. We'll see you soon."

Sean hung up the phone and turned to Peyton. "Everything checks out. Wilder's already at the crime scene, waiting for us."

"Didn't trust me?" Chip asked. Peyton hadn't heard him approach, but now he stood only a few paces away, his eyes gleaming mischievously. "Ah, well," he said, "you can't be too careful with strangers, can you?" He waved them forward. "Come on—time's wasting."

"Where exactly are we going?" Peyton asked, trying to keep her apprehension from tainting her voice as she studied the rickety airboat.

"Deep into the swamps," Chip replied, his gaze locked on the task at hand. "The woman's body's way out there. Gonna be quite the ride." He looked up at her then, a gleam in his eye that made her stomach twist in knots. "But don't you worry, missy. I'm an excellent driver."

CHAPTER FOUR

With a mixture of curiosity and trepidation, Peyton climbed onto the airboat alongside Sean and Chip.

Here goes nothing, she thought.

As the engine roared to life, her mind drifted back to her parents. She imagined her father's eyes lighting up with excitement at the sight of this unique ecosystem, his mind racing with questions and observations to share with her mother. Marie Risk would have been no less fascinated, her artistic sensibilities stirred by the vivid colors and textures that surrounded them. Together, they would have reveled in exploring the unknown terrain, taking countless photographs and collecting samples to study when they returned to their cabin. The swamps, teeming with life and mystery, might have become another cherished destination for the family, much like Eden's Gate National Park in Wyoming.

A sudden lurch pulled Peyton from her thoughts.

Despite Chip's assurance that he was an 'excellent driver,' he seemed determined to throw Peyton from the boat. He drove the airboat fast, zipping through the water with an unnerving disregard for safety. The swamp flew by in a dizzying blur.

Despite the pace, however, Peyton found herself marveling at her surroundings nonetheless. Thick curtains of Spanish moss hung from twisted branches of cypress trees, swaying gently in the breeze. The roots of the trees protruded from the murky water, creating eerie, gnarled formations that seemed to belong to a different era. All around them, the swamp teemed with life: great blue herons waded silently through the shallows, while alligators lounged on floating logs, their eyes watching the intruders warily.

The airboat suddenly skidded to a halt, spraying water and mud in every direction as it came to rest on a small, muddy island nestled deep within the swamps. Dense clusters of cypress trees surrounded the island, while thick walls of palmetto bushes formed an impenetrable barrier around the perimeter. A turtle with colorful markings on its shell slipped into the water, leaving several air bubbles in its wake.

Chip turned the engine off, and in its absence Peyton heard a cacophony of noise: buzzing insects, chirping frogs, birds she couldn't identify. Her gaze was drawn to a second airboat parked nearby, its hull coated in a layer of grime that camouflaged it perfectly with the muddy shoreline.

"This is where the body was found?" she asked, suspecting the second airboat might belong to the officer they were on their way to meet, Dayton Wilder.

"Yep," Chip replied, his eyes scanning the island as if searching for something. "It was a local fisherman who made the discovery. He was out checking his crawfish traps when he noticed something strange tangled up in the roots of one of those old cypress trees. Thought it was just a big ol' gator at first, but when he got closer, he realized it was a woman's body."

Peyton shivered at the thought.

"Was anyone else with him?" Sean asked. He was looking warily over the side of the boat, as if expecting to see a pair of yellow eyes staring back up at him.

"No, just him," Chip said, furrowing his brow as he tried to remember the details. "He called it in right away, though. Said he'd never seen anything like it in all his years living out here."

I should hope not, Peyton thought.

Chip jumped over the side of the airboat, splashing into the mud. "Time's a-wasting!" he said. "Are you two coming, or are you afraid of a few bugs?"

Peyton and Sean exchanged a glance. *What have we gotten ourselves into?* Sean's eyes seemed to say.

Peyton got out of the boat next, followed by Sean. Peyton was grateful for the knee-high boots she'd brought—anything shorter would've been quickly filled with mud.

As they followed Chip across the island, Peyton thought about the fisherman stumbling upon the body as he went about his daily routine, the swamp's murky depths yielding up yet another gruesome secret. What must he have felt at the discovery? And how long had the body been there?

"Here we are," Chip announced, stopping beside a burly, sweaty police officer who was crouched over a set of tracks in the mud. The man looked up at their approach, and Peyton was struck by the intensity of his gaze. His eyes were a piercing shade of blue that seemed to bore straight into her soul, and a jagged scar ran across his left cheek, giving him an air of ruggedness that seemed fitting for someone working in

21

such a harsh environment.

"Dayton Wilder," the officer introduced himself, holding out a hand for them to shake. "I'm the lead investigator on this case."

"Nice to meet you," Sean said, shaking Wilder's hand firmly. "I'm Sean O'Malley, and this is my partner, Peyton Risk."

"Good to have the NPS here," Wilder replied, nodding in acknowledgment before turning his attention back to Chip. "Thanks for bringing them out, Chip. I can take it from here."

"Sure thing, Dayton," Chip said, looking relieved that his part in the investigation was over. "Y'all take care now." With that, he retreated, whistling a jaunty tune.

"Quite a character," Sean said, looking after Chip.

"Who, Chip?" Wilder asked. "Yeah, he's a character alright." A hint of a smile tugged at the corner of his mouth. "Best airboat captain in the county, though."

Peyton studied the officer in front of her for a moment longer. Even in the wilting humidity, he was meticulously professional, with his dark uniform spotless and a silver badge prominently displayed on his chest. He projected an aura of calm authority that Peyton found reassuring.

"Come on," Wilder said, nodding toward a dense thicket of cypress trees. "I'll show you the body."

Peyton and Sean followed him as he carefully picked his way through the swampy terrain, avoiding the gnarled roots and patches of thick mud that threatened to swallow their boots whole. The oppressive humidity weighed down on them like a suffocating blanket, making Peyton's chest feel tight and her breathing labored. Insects buzzed incessantly around them, a constant reminder of the life teeming within the swamps.

As they approached the water's edge, Peyton caught sight of a young woman's lifeless form. She was lying on her back, her long blonde hair tangled with the decaying leaves and debris that littered the shore. Her hazel eyes stared blankly up at the sky, her once-fit, athletic build now marred by bruises and scratches. The vibrant colors of her professional attire were muted by the grime of the swamp, making it seem as though the very essence of her had been drained away.

"Her name is Jennifer Easton," Wilder said quietly, his gaze fixed on the body. "She was a successful marketing consultant from New York City, running her own firm. She came down here to do some research for a client, looking into potential tourism opportunities in the area."

Peyton listened intently, trying to reconcile the image of the confident, ambitious woman described by Wilder with the broken figure before them. Whom had Jennifer met in these swamps? And what could have prompted someone to take her life in such a brutal manner?

"Look at her neck," Peyton said softly, pointing to the visible marks encircling Jennifer's throat. From a distance, they might have appeared to be nothing more than a bit of dried mud, but up close, it was clear that the marks were in fact bruises.

"Those marks..." Sean murmured, crouching down beside her to get a better look. "They don't look like they were made by hands, do they?"

Peyton shook her head, her gaze drawn back to the peculiar pattern of bruises and abrasions that marred Jennifer's skin. The marks were uneven and jagged, as though they'd been caused by something rougher than human fingers. And yet, there was an undeniable symmetry to their placement.

"Almost looks like she was choked with a rope," Peyton mused, her brow furrowed in thought. "But it's not quite right, is it? The pattern is too irregular for a rope."

"Could be some kind of makeshift garrote," Sean suggested, his eyes narrowed as he examined the marks more closely.

"What about a vine?" Peyton said suddenly, looking around at the vines drooping from the trees.

"Possible," Wilder conceded, wiping sweat from his brow. "But it'd have to be strong and flexible enough to not break under the pressure." He glanced around at the surrounding foliage as though expecting the murder weapon to reveal itself.

"Whatever it was, it looks like the killer knew what he was doing," Sean said grimly. "I don't see much for defensive wounds. Then again, it's tough to tell, since we don't know how long she was in the water or how else she might have gotten these cuts and bruises on her arms." Sean gestured to the injuries he was talking about.

Peyton nodded, feeling a chill run down her spine despite the humid air. Whoever had done this had been cold, methodical, and utterly ruthless—a dangerous combination that only made her more determined to see justice served.

At that moment, a shrill voice cut through the heavy silence of the swamp, startling Peyton out of her thoughts. "Hey! Get away from her!"

Peyton jerked upright, her heart pounding as she looked up to see a woman striding toward them, her face contorted with anger.

CHAPTER FIVE

The woman appeared to be in her mid-thirties, with auburn hair pulled back in a tight bun and sharp green eyes that didn't miss a thing. Her clothes were simple but elegant – a white blouse tucked into beige slacks – and she moved with an air of authority that made it clear she was not someone to be trifled with.

"I said," the woman repeated, "step away from the body."

Peyton stared, unsure what to do. Who was this person, and what made her think she had the right to tell them what to do?

Just as Peyton was about to speak, Wilder stepped forward, looking a bit embarrassed. "Ranger Risk, Ranger O'Malley," he said, "this is Dr. Rita Silver, our coroner around here." He smiled uneasily. "We're all on the same team."

"Team or no team, I gave explicit instructions about preserving the crime scene," Dr. Rita Silver said crisply, stopping a few feet away from Jennifer's body. She cast a disapproving glance at Wilder, who wilted under her glance.

"We haven't touched her," Peyton said. "We're trained professionals. We were only observing—we wouldn't compromise the scene."

"Observation should be done at an appropriate distance. You could be contaminating potential evidence without knowing," Dr. Silver retorted, her eyes flickering between Peyton and Sean.

Sean gave Peyton a glance as if to say, *Someone woke up on the wrong side of the bed.*

Sean stepped back, and Peyton followed suit, though she couldn't help but feel frustrated by the dismissiveness of Dr. Silver.

She's just concerned about contamination, Peyton reminded herself. *Like Wilder said, we're all on the same team.*

Peyton watched as Dr. Silver donned a pair of latex gloves and began her examination of the body with methodical precision. The sunlight filtering through the trees cast dappled shadows across the scene, highlighting the contrast between the vibrant swamp surrounding them and the lifeless form of Jennifer Easton. The sounds of distant wildlife created an eerie backdrop to the somber investigation, reminding Peyton just how wild this part of the country was.

She glanced over at Sean, who stood by quietly, his gaze fixed on Dr. Silver's every movement. They both knew better than to interrupt the coroner at work, but it was clear they shared the same burning curiosity about the case.

"Dr. Silver?" Peyton ventured cautiously, unable to contain her questions any longer. "I couldn't help but notice the unusual marks on the victim's neck. Were the other three victims killed in a similar manner?"

Dr. Silver paused briefly, her eyes flickering from the corpse to Peyton for a moment before returning to her task. "Yes," she replied curtly, her attention clearly still on the body. "They were all killed in a similar way. It's difficult to tell what was used to strangle the victims— it might've been hemp."

"Actually," Peyton said, "I was wondering if it might have been a vine."

The coroner paused in her examination, looking up at Peyton with surprise. The intensity of her gaze softened ever so slightly, replaced by a begrudging respect. "It's possible," Dr. Silver admitted. "The markings on the victims' necks are consistent with something pliable and strong, like a vine."

Sean scratched his chin, his blue eyes thoughtful. "Why would the killer use a vine, though?" he mused aloud. He looked to Peyton, Wilder, and Dr. Silver, seeking their input.

Peyton considered the question, her brow furrowing. "Perhaps the killer is intimately familiar with the swamp and knows how to utilize its resources to his advantage. It could also be a way of blending in, making it harder for us to trace the murder weapon."

Wilder chimed in, his words tinged with a thick Louisiana drawl. "Could be some sort of ritual or symbolism, too. You know how these serial killers like to leave their mark." He glanced at the body, his face unreadable but for the faintest flicker of sorrow in his eyes.

Dr. Silver pursed her lips, clearly disliking the attention that had been drawn to her work. Nevertheless, she offered her own thoughts. "It may serve multiple purposes. Using a vine allows the killer to avoid purchasing a weapon that could be traced back to them. It also adds an element of challenge, as if they're taunting us with their ability to use the environment itself as a means of murder."

Peyton walked over to a nearby vine hanging from a tree. "What type of vine is this, anyway?" She didn't recognize it.

Wilder pushed his hat back slightly on his head and squinted at the vine Peyton was holding. "That's a serpent vine," he said, rubbing his chin thoughtfully. "Strong, pliable, and common in these parts. Also known to be poisonous if ingested."

Peyton nodded, mentally storing this information in case it should prove useful later on.

"Anything else you can tell us about the body, Dr. Silver?" Sean asked.

"In the two minutes I've had to examine the body?" Dr. Silver asked, arching an eyebrow. "The bottom line is I won't know more until I've performed a detailed autopsy. However, I can tell you that there is no indication of sexual assault and no sign of any struggle."

Sean nodded, jotting down notes as Peyton turned the vine over and over in her hands. The idea that something as simple as a vine could be used to kill was unsettling.

Then Wilder spoke up again. "If we're dealing with someone who knows the swamp well, could be he's from around here." He looked from Sean to Peyton, his eyes narrow, his southern accent deepening with the seriousness of his words. "Could be he's one of our own."

"Does anyone come to mind?" Peyton asked.

Wilder shook his head. "Not at first blush. I'll think about it, though, let you know if I think of anyone who fits the bill."

"Another thing," Dr. Silver said, suddenly looking up from the body. "This victim was heavily intoxicated, unlike the previous ones."

"How can you tell?" Sean asked.

"Besides the odor of alcohol? There are traces of vomit in her teeth. Her eyes, too, are unusually dilated. I'd say she was quite drunk when she was killed. Black-out drunk, maybe."

Peyton exchanged glances with Sean and Wilder, taking note of this new piece of information.

"Could she have been drugged?" Wilder asked. "Maybe something was slipped into her drink?"

"It's possible," Dr. Silver said. "I won't be able to answer that with any certainty until we run a toxicology test."

"So where was she drinking?" Sean asked, thinking aloud. "Any bars in the area?"

Wilder scratched his unshaven chin, pondering for a moment. "There's the Bayou Saloon near the old mill."

Dr. Silver shook her head, a strand of her dark hair falling across her face. "No, this woman wouldn't have stopped there." She gestured toward the victim's fashionable clothes and stylish makeup, which was now heavily smudged. "She's young, fashionable—I'd bet she was looking for a more lively spot to enjoy herself."

"Then where?" Peyton asked, her brow furrowed in concentration.

"Gator's Den," Dr. Silver replied without hesitation. "It's the only place around here that caters to a younger crowd, not to mention tourists. They serve all kinds of specialty cocktails and have a reputation for attracting twenty-something partygoers."

"Gator's Den, huh?" Wilder echoed, nodding. "Makes sense. I've been inside a time or two to break up a fight. Mostly, though, it's a quiet place."

"Quiet can be dangerous, too," Peyton murmured, wondering if that bar was where Jennifer had met her killer. Had someone followed her out of the bar or perhaps slipped something into her drink and kidnapped her?

And if so, might there be someone who had witnessed it?

CHAPTER SIX

The shovel chipped at the root, peeling back the bark to reveal the white, flesh-like wood underneath.

Like a woman's skin, the man thought, pausing to wipe sweat from his brow. Now that he thought about it, it felt very much like he was chopping through an arm, perhaps dismembering a body so he could feed it to the gators. That was a method he had never tried before. It might be worth considering, however.

The man finally finished chopping through the root, then ripped it out of the hole. "Sorry," he muttered, casting the root aside. He leaned on the shovel for a moment, peering around, suddenly self-conscious.

You're safe, he told himself, trying to swallow and discovering that his mouth was as sticky as a tar pit. *No one followed you. You made sure of it.*

The man took a deep breath, drawing strength and solace from his surroundings. The murky waters of the swamp reflected the golden sunlight, creating an otherworldly glow that seemed to dance on the surface. Insects buzzed and chirped all around him, their voices providing a soothing soundtrack that relaxed his mind.

He reveled in the strange beauty of this place, feeling a connection to the dark corners of the world where nature remained untamed and unforgiving. Here, away from civilization, he felt truly at home.

As the hole grew deeper, the man's thoughts wandered back to his most recent kill. He could still hear her screams echoing in his ears, her desperate pleas for mercy that had only served to fuel his lust for power. He recalled how her eyes had widened in terror when she realized what was about to happen, and a shiver of ecstasy shot through him at the memory.

He paused his work again, his hand absently tracing a spider-like vein in the wood of the handle. He could remember *her* veins, too. As pale as moonlight in the dim glow of the swamp's lanterns.

She had been like a moth to the flame, and he'd been more than happy to accommodate her last flight. He basked in the thought of their final struggle, how the realization of her fate illuminated her eyes brighter than the neon lights of that bar ever did.

Oh, how he savored the memory. He cherished the fear in her eyes, the panic in her voice, and the futile struggle against his grip. It was intoxicating—a high that no drug or drink could ever compare to.

But now it was over, and he was left with an insatiable craving for more. He clenched his fists, his grimy nails digging into his palms, as he fought to keep himself under control.

No, he thought, warning himself. *It's not time yet. I need to lay low. I need to be smart about this.*

The man picked up his shovel and continued digging. "Almost done," he muttered under his breath, tossing aside another shovelful of damp earth.

Once the hole was several feet deep, the man set the shovel aside and reached into his pocket, pulling out a pair of earrings, a waterlogged cell phone, and a necklace. The earrings were small, delicate, and adorned with tiny sapphires, their silvery surface now tarnished from exposure to the swamp's murky waters. The cell phone was cracked and lifeless, its screen shattered beyond recognition.

He tossed the earrings and the cell phone into the hole without hesitation. But as he held the necklace in his hand, a sudden reluctance washed over him. There was something about this particular memento that gave him pause.

The man felt the smoothness of the wood and the coolness of the amber between his fingers as he remembered the woman's screams and how she had pleaded for her life. He had felt so powerful in that moment, controlling her fate as certainly as if he were far more than a mere mortal. The memory sent a shudder of ecstasy through him.

Why can't I keep it? he thought, fingering the necklace. *No one will ever know, will they?*

His fingers danced along the amber pendant, its warmth comforting him, connecting him back to her. It was his power incarnate, his macabre love letter to a woman whose life he'd drained out of her.

The hesitation stretched out, a single moment ballooned into a seemingly limitless expanse of time. His hand hovered over the hole for an eternity as he wrestled with himself. The necklace held a power over him, a connection to the life he had snuffed out and the thrill of the hunt that he so desperately craved.

If someone sees you with it...

Then, on impulse, he slipped the necklace around his neck and tucked it beneath his shirt. *Who's going to see it?* he asked himself. *It's not even visible.*

He hesitated a few moments longer, unaware that he'd already made his decision. Then, unwilling to take the necklace off, he picked up the shovel and began filling in the hole.

"Nobody will ever see it. Nobody will ever know," he repeated under his breath like a mantra. As dirt cascaded onto the buried earrings and the waterlogged cell phone, the man's heart raced, pumping adrenaline through his veins, further heightening the thrill of his deception.

Once the hole was covered, he took a moment to survey his handiwork. It looked undisturbed, just another patch of earth amidst the swampy island. To ensure the concealment was complete, he scattered debris – broken twigs, damp leaves, and clumps of moss – across the newly turned soil.

"Perfect," he whispered, a smile curving at the corner of his lips.

Satisfied that his trophies were safely hidden away, the man hoisted the shovel over his shoulder and began walking. The ground squelched beneath his boots, the mud sucking at him with each stride, threatening to pull him down into its dark embrace. He did not mind, however, no more than he minded the biting insects or the humidity. This was his world, his sanctuary. His hunting ground.

And he was the predator that stalked it.

As he moved farther away, the forest closed in around him, a thick wall of foliage and shadows, his footprints erased by the marshy terrain. His own personal Eden, untouched by the civilized world.

As he continued his trek, the verdant foliage grew thicker. The sweet scent of blooming magnolias mingled with the earthy aroma of decaying leaves, creating a heady perfume that threatened to overwhelm him. The sun cast dappled shadows through the tangled canopy above, playing tricks on his vision as light and darkness danced together in an endless waltz.

Finally reaching the edge of the island, he spotted his airboat waiting patiently among the cattails and lily pads. He climbed aboard, feeling the familiar sway of the vessel beneath him as he stowed the shovel and took his seat at the helm. A flick of his wrist brought the engine to life, its low rumble reverberating through the swamp like a predator's growl.

"Time to go," he murmured, gripping the throttle tightly.

The airboat glided smoothly across the swamp, its fan propelling it through the murky waters. The man's fingers grazed the necklace hidden beneath his shirt, sending a shiver of anticipation down his spine as he remembered each of his four kills.

Nothing compares to the thrill of the hunt, he thought, his eyes taking in the tangled beauty of the swamp around him. *It's like playing God, deciding who lives and who dies.*

And soon, he believed, it would be time for another to give up their life.

CHAPTER SEVEN

Peyton was still thinking about the marks around Jennifer Easton's neck as she and Sean arrived at the Gator's Den. The bar, a floating dock that had been transformed into a watering hole, was nestled in the heart of the swamps, surrounded by boats of various shapes and sizes. Some were small skiffs, while others were larger vessels, all moored alongside the rickety wooden structure. The air was thick with the scent of stale beer and the distant hum of laughter and conversation.

After Wilder had brought Peyton and Sean back to the precinct on his airboat, he had lent them an unmarked Jeep for the duration of their investigation. The vehicle was a godsend, allowing them to navigate the labyrinthine shoreline and dense foliage with relative ease.

"Quite the unique place," Sean remarked, looking around at the eclectic mix of patrons milling about on the dock. "I can see why it would have some appeal for the younger crowd."

Peyton nodded, watching as the back door opened and a man in dirty coveralls tossed a bucket of gray water across the wooden boards. "Maybe she was trying to blend in with the locals so she could see what tourism opportunities there are in this area."

"It's exotic, alright," Sean said. "For someone like me, growing up in Montana?" He shook his head. "This is an entirely different world."

"Pretty different from Virginia, too," Peyton said. "What do you say we head in and see if anyone can tell us about Jennifer?"

Peyton and Sean stepped out of the unmarked Jeep and approached the entrance to the floating dock bar.

"Quite the eclectic crowd," Peyton murmured, scanning the assortment of vessels. She could see people lounging on deck chairs, nursing hangovers from the night before. The air was thick with the scent of stale beer, cigarette smoke, and the faint tang of saltwater.

"Seems like a place where anything goes," Sean said, his eyes narrowing as he observed the patrons milling about the dock.

As they entered the bar, the atmosphere shifted from lazy morning lethargy to something more akin to a predator's den. The interior was dimly lit, with shadows pooling in the corners and a haze of smoke hovering over the room. A long wooden bar stretched along one wall, its surface marred by countless scratches and stains. Behind it, an assortment of liquor bottles glinted in the low light, their contents promising oblivion and escape.

The patrons themselves were an interesting mix—grizzled locals nursing early morning drinks, hipster-types nursing artisanal coffee and sporting tattoos and piercings, and a few younger men who looked like they hadn't slept in days. As Peyton surveyed the scene, she noticed a couple of them hastily stashing small baggies into their pockets, their movements furtive and nervous.

"They're lucky we've got better things to do than bust them," Sean murmured to Peyton.

Peyton nodded and turned her attention to the bartender, hoping that he might have seen Jennifer here. She wove through the maze of tables and chairs, Sean right behind her. But as they approached the bar, the bartender's gaze locked onto them, instantly wary. He was a tall, thin man with a scruffy beard and a stained apron. His eyes were bloodshot, and his expression soured as he took in their appearance.

"Sorry, we don't serve cops," he growled, his voice rough and gravelly.

Peyton's jaw tightened, her frustration simmering beneath the surface. She was ready to give the bartender a piece of her mind, but Sean spoke first.

Ignoring the bartender's blatant hostility, Sean said, "We just need to ask if anyone saw a young woman here last night by the name of Jennifer Easton." He held up his phone, displaying a picture of Jennifer—her blonde hair cascading over her shoulders, hazel eyes bright and confident. "She was killed, and we're just trying to find justice for her."

The room seemed to hold its breath as people exchanged wary glances, the tension thickening in the air. Peyton felt her heart race, acutely aware of how unwelcome they were in this place.

From a nearby table, a bald, heavyset man with a beard that nearly reached his chest rose to his feet. His biceps strained against the fabric of his faded black t-shirt as he approached them, a scowl etched across his features. With each step, the wooden floor creaked under his considerable weight.

"Must be hard of hearing," the man grumbled, planting himself directly in front of Sean. His breath reeked of stale alcohol and cigarettes, making Peyton's stomach churn. "Y'all ain't welcome here. Best you leave now."

Peyton's hands itched to reach for her sidearm, but she forced herself to remain still, sensing that any sudden moves could escalate the situation. She tried to think of a way to defuse the tension without resorting to force. She knew that finding the truth about Jennifer's death hinged on their ability to navigate the delicate politics of this insular community, but it was becoming increasingly difficult to maintain her composure.

"Look, we don't want any trouble," Sean said calmly, meeting the man's gaze without flinching. "We just need some information. That's all."

"Information?" the man sneered, narrowing his eyes at the picture of Jennifer on Sean's phone. "Well, ain't that a shame. You two come waltzing in here like you own the place, expecting us to help you? We don't take kindly to strangers, especially not law enforcement."

"Did you see her?" Peyton asked. "You look like you've been drinking here all night."

The man rounded on her, narrowing his eyes. "What's that supposed to mean?"

"It's just a question," Sean said, his voice low and controlled as he stared directly into the heavyset man's eyes. "This doesn't have to be complicated."

The bald man's face reddened, the veins in his forehead bulging with barely restrained anger. "You're lucky I don't knock that smug look right off your face," he snarled, looming over Sean like a predator sizing up its prey. The tension in the air became palpable, the rest of the bar's patrons silently watching the confrontation unfold.

Sean's jaw tightened, but he refused to back down. As an experienced NPS agent, he knew when to push and when to retreat—and this was no time for retreat. "Let's stick to the subject," he said, ignoring the threat. "Were you here last night or not?"

The heavyset man crossed his arms. "And why the hell should I tell you?"

At that moment, Peyton's gaze drifted away from the standoff, her attention drawn to a young waitress at the back of the room. The woman was clearing a table, but her movements were erratic, almost frantic, as if she were desperate to avoid drawing attention to herself. Her hands shook visibly, causing silverware to clatter against the plates she was gathering.

Peyton studied the waitress intently, an instinctive feeling telling her that there was more to this woman than met the eye. Their gazes locked briefly, and Peyton sensed a flicker of fear in the woman's eyes before she quickly looked away. With a furtive glance around the room, the waitress scooped up the stack of dishes and hurried into the kitchen, nearly tripping on a customer's leg and spilling the dishes.

"And if you'd like to take this outside—" Sean was saying in a polite tone. Peyton grabbed his arm before he could finish.

"This isn't worth it," she said, her eyes on the doorway through which the waitress had retreated. "Let's just get out of here. We can come back another time."

Sean tore his gaze away from the heavyset man, confusion etched across his face. "What are you talking about?"

"Trust me," Peyton said, looking into his eyes and willing him to understand. "It's not worth it."

"Go on," the heavyset man said in a taunting voice. "Listen to your lady friend."

Reluctant to leave with the situation unresolved, Sean hesitated for a moment before finally sighing. "Alright," he said. Then he cast the heavyset man a warning look. "But we'll be back." His eyes were troubled, however, and Peyton could tell he still didn't know what was going on.

He'll understand soon enough, she thought.

The heavyset man grunted as Peyton and Sean made their way through the jeering crowd of patrons toward the exit. "Come back as often as you like!" he called, clearly pleased he had won. "We'll roll out the red carpet for you."

Sean looked ready to respond to this, but Peyton grabbed his arm and shook her head at him. "It's not worth it," she said.

Outside, the air was thick with humidity, the sounds of the swamp drifting on the breeze. Sean turned to Peyton, whose annoyance was evident.

"You shouldn't have interfered," he said, his voice tight. "I could've handled that guy."

"I know you could have," Peyton replied calmly. "But there's a better way to get the answers we need."

He stared at her. "What are you talking about?"

She tipped her head to the side, indicating that he should follow her. "Come on—I'll show you."

Without waiting for a response, she led him around the side of the building. There, hidden from view, was a door to the kitchen. To their surprise, the nervous waitress she'd observed earlier was leaning

36

against the wall, smoking a cigarette with trembling hands.

The woman's eyes widened with alarm when she saw them approaching, her dark hair sticking to her damp forehead. She looked like a cornered animal, desperate for escape, but Peyton held up her hands in a placating gesture.

"Hey, it's okay," she said softly. "We just want to talk."

"Who are you?" the waitress asked, her eyes darting between them. The name tag on her uniform read 'BETSY.'

"Ranger Peyton Risk," she replied, gesturing to herself, then to Sean. "And this is my partner, Ranger Sean O'Malley. We're investigating the death of Jennifer Easton. We don't want any trouble; we just need some information."

Betsy hesitated, clearly weighing her options. She took one last drag from her cigarette before flicking it away into the murky water below. As the smoke curled and dissipated into the humid air, she finally spoke.

"What do you want to know?" she asked.

Peyton's eyes scanned Betsy's anxious face, taking in the beads of sweat that clung to her forehead despite the shade provided by the building. The smoky scent from the cigarette lingered in the air, mingling with the earthy aroma of the surrounding swamp. Peyton softened her tone as she attempted to calm the waitress.

"For starters," she said, "can you tell us if you recognize her?" Peyton gestured to Sean, and he held up his phone, showing Betsy a picture of Jennifer.

Betsy hesitated, her fingers drumming against her thigh in a nervous rhythm. She glanced over her shoulder at the kitchen door behind her before turning back to face Peyton. "I...I saw her," Betsy admitted quietly, her voice barely audible above the hum of insects in the dense foliage around them. "Jennifer was here last night."

"What else do you remember?" Sean asked.

Betsy shifted her weight from one foot to the other, pulling at the hem of her apron. "I didn't really pay much attention to her, if I'm honest. It was a busy night." She paused, her gaze drifting toward the water's edge. "But I did notice she had quite a bit to drink. Seemed like she was trying to fit in, make friends with the locals or something."

Peyton absorbed Betsy's words, her mind weaving the details into the tapestry of Jennifer's final hours. She imagined the young woman navigating the crowded bar, laughing too loudly at jokes she didn't understand, attempting to bridge the gap between her city-slicker

37

upbringing and the gritty reality of the swamp people. "Did she seem upset or agitated in any way?" Peyton asked.

Betsy shook her head, strands of hair escaping from the loose bun atop her head. "Not that I could tell. But like I said, I wasn't paying too much attention."

Peyton's brow furrowed as she considered their next move. Though Betsy's information was limited, it served to further humanize Jennifer, painting a picture of a young woman adrift in unfamiliar territory. What had brought her to this bar? And what events had transpired between her last drink and her untimely death?

"Did you recognize anyone Jennifer was with?" Sean asked.

Betsy hesitated before nodding slowly. "There was one guy she seemed pretty close to. His name is Hal Reddish. They were laughing and flirting all night. I saw them sharing a few drinks at the bar, whispering in each other's ears, dancing together—that kind of thing. It looked like they were really into one another."

Peyton exchanged a glance with Sean, who raised an eyebrow in silent acknowledgment of this new piece of information. She turned back to Betsy. "How do you know Reddish?" she asked.

"Everyone around here knows him," Betsy replied, her voice tinged with distaste. "It's a tight-knit community, and he's been a part of it since we were kids. We went to high school together."

"You sound like you don't think very highly of him."

"No one does," Betsy scoffed. "He was the bad boy everyone warned you about but couldn't resist. He'd sell drugs at school, get into fights, and was constantly suspended. The teachers were afraid of him, and so were most of the students."

Peyton's eyes narrowed as she processed Betsy's words. "What about his relationships with women?" she asked.

"Reddish never took no for an answer," Betsy said, her expression darkening. "He could be incredibly pushy and manipulative. I've heard stories about girls who tried to reject him, only for him to turn nasty and violent." She bit her lip and glanced away, and Peyton had the impression that Betsy had probably been one of those girls.

"Did Jennifer leave with him?" Sean asked, cutting straight to the heart of the matter.

Betsy nodded, her face pale. "Yeah, they left together," she said. But then she added quickly, "But that doesn't mean he did anything to her. I mean, Hal's a jerk, but I never thought he'd be capable of...you know."

"Murder?" Peyton said bluntly. Betsy winced in response, but didn't deny it.

"Exactly," she said. "She was clearly from out of state – she kept talking about some marketing consultancy firm up in New York City – so that probably caught Hal's eye. He likes shiny things, you know? Novelty." She bit at one of her chipped nails and looked away.

As helpful as all this information was, Peyton had the impression that Betsy was still holding something back. She wanted to avoid pushing Betsy too hard, but not at the expense of catching a killer.

"Is there something more you'd like to tell us about him?" Peyton asked gently, her voice low and non-threatening.

Betsy swallowed hard, glancing around nervously before leaning in closer. "The worst part is, last I knew, Hal was part of a white supremacy group. They go by the name 'Delta Dawn.' They're trouble, real trouble. They've been known to harass people, vandalize property, and even worse."

"You got any idea where we might find them?" Sean asked.

"Wait," Betsy interrupted, her voice trembling slightly. "I'll tell you, but you have to promise not to mention my name, okay? I don't want them coming after me or my family."

Peyton met the young woman's fearful gaze and nodded solemnly. "We promise, your name won't be mentioned."

"Alright, then." Betsy sighed, lowering her voice even further. "They have a sort of...hangout. It's an old preschool near the edge of town, down by the river."

"What's the name of this school?" Sean asked.

"Beckwith, I think. Used to be a great place but now—" She shrugged. "You know how it goes. The world moves on."

"Thank you, Betsy," Peyton said, meeting the waitress's gaze once more. "Your help means a lot to us."

Betsy hesitated, biting her lip.

"Is there something more we should know?" Peyton asked.

"Just be careful," Betsy said. "They're certain to be armed, and if they see law enforcement approaching...well, if they think they can make you disappear, they just might do it to keep you from discovering whatever they've been up to."

CHAPTER EIGHT

Peyton and Sean pulled up to the old, run-down preschool, its walls marred by chipped paint and covered in a chaotic array of graffiti. A group of tough-looking men loitered out front, their eyes darting around as if expecting trouble. One man leaned against the wall, flicking the ashes from his cigarette onto the cracked pavement. Another stood nearby, arms crossed over his chest, occasionally barking terse orders at the third, who paced back and forth like a caged animal.

"Think they're armed?" Peyton murmured, studying the men from the safety of their vehicle, parked far enough away to avoid detection.

"Definitely," Sean replied, his eyes narrowing as he assessed the situation. "The question is, what kind of weapons?" He gestured toward the pacing man, whose bulky jacket obscured the details of whatever lay beneath. "Could be guns or knives. Maybe both."

Beckwith Preschool was a sad remnant of its former self, a weary structure sagging beneath the weight of years of neglect. Vines crept along the outer walls, weaving their way through broken windows and into darkened classrooms. The playground, once filled with the laughter of children, now stood silent, the rusted swings swaying gently in the breeze.

The surrounding area was equally desolate, a barren wasteland of cracked streets and boarded-up buildings. It was clear that this part of town had been forgotten, left to wither and rot under the relentless Louisiana sun. Even the trees seemed to have given up, their gnarled limbs reaching out like skeletal fingers in a futile attempt to escape their fate.

"This place gives me the creeps," Peyton whispered. "It's like something out of a horror movie."

"Or Chernobyl," Sean said, his gaze never leaving the men in front of the school.

"So what's our plan?" Peyton asked.

"We could try a direct approach," he suggested. "Confront them head-on. They might respect that."

Peyton raised an eyebrow, memories of their near-fight at the bar still fresh in her mind. "You're just spoiling for a fight, aren't you?"

He shrugged innocently. "What can I say? I could use the exercise." He started cracking his knuckles.

"And if we do that," Peyton said, "we'll probably spook Reddish, assuming he's inside."

"Unless he's one of these three jokers."

"It's possible. But I don't want to make any assumptions."

Sean sighed. "What's your idea, then?"

"We detour around, see if we can't find another way in. It's a school, after all—there should be plenty of windows."

"Fine, fine," Sean said, clearly disappointed.

The two of them cautiously exited their vehicle, taking care to stay out of sight as they approached the school. The building was a sad, decaying monument to lost hopes and dreams, its once-vibrant exterior now faded and marked with graffiti. The windows were cracked or shattered, and the roof sagged under the weight of years of neglect.

As they drew closer, Peyton could hear faint sounds coming from inside the school—laughter, cursing, and the occasional crash of glass on concrete. It seemed that the place had become a haven for those seeking refuge on society's fringes.

Moving stealthily, Peyton and Sean crept along the side of the building, careful to avoid stepping on any debris that might give away their presence. As they rounded a corner, Peyton spotted a high window, partially obscured by overgrown vines.

"Look," she whispered, pointing to the window. "If you give me a boost, I think I can get up there."

"Are you sure?" Sean asked, concern etched on his face. "It's pretty high up, and those vines don't look too stable."

"I'm positive," Peyton replied. "Just give me a hand, and I'll do the rest."

With a nod, Sean positioned himself under the window, cupping his hands for Peyton to step into. As Sean lifted her upward, Peyton reached out to grasp the edge of the window, her fingers digging into the crumbling concrete. She hoisted herself up, praying that the decaying structure would hold long enough for her to make it inside.

"Your turn," Peyton said, turning around to help Sean up. "Just give me your hand and—" She stopped short as she noticed the pair of figures ambling toward Sean. One was tall and lanky, with the sunken features of a heroin addict; the other was stockier, with a brutish, pockmarked face.

Both of them were holding knives.

"Well, well," the stocky one said, "look what we have here." He looked Sean up and down, then flicked his eyes toward Peyton. "NPS, huh?" he said. "What's that stand for? You some kind of cleaning company?"

The lanky man sniggered. "Janitors, probably. Don't realize this school ain't been running for five years now."

Peyton crouched, ready to drop back down to Sean, but he glanced up at her and waved her back. "Go on," he said. "I'll keep these fellas occupied."

Peyton hesitated, her fingers gripping the window ledge tightly while her instincts screamed at her to drop down and help her partner. For a moment, time seemed to slow as she weighed the decision. She knew that if she stayed, they would lose their element of surprise, and there was a good chance Reddish would hear the fight and get away. Yet leaving Sean alone against two armed men went against every fiber of her being.

"Go!" Sean said again, more urgently this time. Peyton could see the resolve in his eyes, and she had the impression he'd be angry with her if she didn't stick to the plan.

"Where you going, little birdie?" the stocky one called. "Don't want to stay and play?"

Trusting in Sean's ability to handle himself, Peyton took a deep breath and pushed herself through the window, dropping down on the other side.

As her feet landed on the creaky floorboards inside the old school, Peyton heard Sean address the two men. She couldn't hear the words, but she *could* hear the note of bravado in his voice. *Be careful, Sean,* she thought, hoping she hadn't just made a terrible mistake. *Don't underestimate them.*

Peyton closed her eyes for a second, sending silent words of encouragement and support to Sean before steeling herself for what lay ahead. The air inside the school was stale, heavy with the scent of decay and dampness.

She moved cautiously through the darkened hallways, her eyes scanning the peeling paint and broken doors for any sign of Hal Reddish. Each step echoed in the eerie silence, punctuated only by the occasional drip of water from the leaking roof. In the dim light, the shadows seemed to dance and contort into grotesque shapes, threatening to swallow her whole.

"Where are you, Reddish?" she whispered under her breath.

Classroom doors hung crookedly on their hinges, some barely clinging to the decaying woodwork. Desks and chairs lay overturned, long forgotten by the children who once occupied them. The entire building seemed to groan with the weight of its own neglect, a testament to the decay that had taken root in this forsaken place.

Peyton tiptoed through the darkened hallways, avoiding the creaking floorboards and the crunch of broken glass underfoot. As she turned a corner, she spotted a faint glow emanating from a slightly ajar door at the end of the corridor. Carefully, she approached, unease prickling at her skin. With one hand on her sidearm, Peyton nudged the door open farther, revealing a room bathed in flickering candlelight.

A man lay sprawled across a stained mattress, his eyes closed and a thin trail of drool escaping the corner of his mouth. His thin frame was covered in tattoos and mottled bruises, evidence of a life lived hard and fast. A burnt spoon and a syringe lay discarded on the floor beside him.

"Are you Hal Reddish?" Peyton asked in a low voice, her fingers still resting on her weapon.

The man's eyelids fluttered open, revealing bloodshot eyes that seemed to float in a sea of viscous fluid. He smiled languidly and slurred, "That's my name, don't wear it out."

Peyton studied his face, noting the hollow cheeks and the dark circles under his eyes. This was clearly a man who had surrendered himself to the depths of addiction. Was it his way of coping with the guilt of murder?

"Listen, Hal," she said, "I know you were at the Gator's Den last night with Jennifer Easton. What happened after you left?"

Reddish blinked slowly, his gaze drifting around the room as if trying to latch onto something solid in his foggy mind. "Jennifer?" he murmured, his brow furrowing. "Oh yeah, we were at a bar...I think."

"Did you leave the bar together?" Peyton pressed, trying to maintain her patience as she watched Reddish's thoughts drift further away.

"Yes..." he mumbled, his eyelids growing heavy once more. "Then we had a big argument... She wanted to go somewhere, but I didn't want to... Too tired..."

"Where did she want to go?"

"Swamp... She wanted me to take her there for some marketing thing. But I was tired," Reddish replied, rubbing at his eyes as if trying to wake himself up. "Didn't want to go."

Peyton clenched her fists, forcing herself to remain calm. This was delicate work, extracting information from someone in Reddish's state. "Alright, so you didn't go with her. What did you do after leaving Jennifer?"

"Um..." Reddish's face scrunched up in concentration, sweat beading on his forehead. "Went to a friend's place, played some poker... Drank more. Uh, my buddy Kevin was there, and his girlfriend... Tina? Yeah, Tina."

"Did anyone else see you there?" Peyton asked, trying to piece together a possible alibi for Reddish.

"Sure, lots of people. Must've been...six, seven others?" Reddish said, scratching his head. "We were pretty loud, neighbors complained."

As much as she disliked having to believe the words of a man who seemed barely capable of stringing a sentence together, Peyton couldn't deny that his alibi sounded convincing. She doubted he had the clarity to invent these details on the spot, given his mental state. If the alibi held up, then Reddish wasn't the one responsible for Jennifer's disappearance. But that left her with another question.

If not Reddish, then who? Had Jennifer found someone else to take her into the swamps?

"Where exactly did she want to go?" Peyton asked.

Reddish closed his eyes. Peyton nudged him. "Come on, Hal. Talk to me."

"Ah, yeah," Reddish mumbled, his eyes peeling open. "She was all excited about some haunted island. Wanted me to take her there. But I wasn't into that spooky stuff, you know?"

Haunted island? Peyton thought. *Is he just pulling my leg?*

"Where is this island?" she asked.

Reddish's eyelids began to droop again, his words slurring as the drugs coursing through his system threatened to pull him under once more. "Dunno…somewhere out there…" He trailed off, his head lolling forward.

Frustration surged through Peyton at this sudden dead end. She reached out and shook Reddish by the shoulders, trying to keep him awake long enough to get the information she needed. "Come on, Hal. Focus. Where is the island? Tell me."

"Ah, it's…it's a secret." Reddish giggled, his drug-addled brain finding amusement in the answer. He swayed slightly, his eyelids fluttering closed before snapping open one last time. "If you don't know...you don't deserve to know." With that, he finally succumbed to the effects of the drugs, collapsing onto the filthy mattress with a heavy sigh.

"Hal. Hal!" Peyton shook him, but there was no response.

Just then, Peyton heard approaching footsteps. She spun around, drawing her weapon and aiming it at the doorway just as Sean entered the room. There were streaks of dirt on his clothes, but otherwise he looked unharmed.

Peyton lowered her gun. "I see you did alright," she said, relieved. "Where are your new friends?"

Sean jabbed a thumb over his shoulder. "They're taking a timeout. Won't be joining us any time soon."

Peyton was impressed. She'd known Sean could handle himself in a fight, but the confident way he'd taken on two armed opponents...it was sexy, she had to admit.

Sean nodded his head at the figure on the bed. "Is that Reddish?"

"Unfortunately, yes. He's taking a timeout, too."

"You think he's our guy?"

Peyton shook her head, pressing her lips together in disappointment. "Probably not. He said Jennifer wanted him to take her to some haunted island, but he refused. Then they parted ways."

"Haunted island?" Sean grunted. "You believe him?"

"I don't know what to make about the haunted island part, but one thing seems sure. Jennifer found someone to take her into the swamps...and that person had no intention of bringing her back out."

CHAPTER NINE

"Alright," Peyton said, rubbing wearily at her face. "Let's go over everything again."

She and Sean were sitting in a conference room in a quiet precinct in Louisiana. It was early afternoon, and the air inside the room was heavy and stifling. The AC didn't work, so there were fans running, but they did little to alleviate the sweltering heat. For the first time since arriving in Louisiana, Peyton really missed the fresh mountain air of her cabin.

In the rest of the precinct, officers moved about their business with quiet efficiency. Some typed away at their computers, while others murmured into phones or spoke softly to one another. Despite the oppressive heat, there was a sense of purpose in the air, a determination to see justice served, and Peyton found herself admiring the professionalism of these officers.

The pictures and details of all four victims were tacked to a wall. Peyton stared at the pictures, trying to figure out what connected them. Had they been targeted for a specific reason, or had they simply been in the wrong place at the wrong time?

"Maybe we should take a break, clear our heads," suggested Sean. "We've been at this a while now."

Peyton could hear the weariness in her partner's tone, and she understood where he was coming from. Her eyes were tired, making it difficult to focus, and taking a break was often a good way to get a fresh perspective.

Then again, the clock was always ticking, and there was no telling when another body might show up.

"I'm not quite ready yet," she replied. "There has to be some reason why these people were chosen, and I want to find out what it is."

Sean sighed but didn't protest. Perhaps he knew that protesting would do no good.

Peyton turned her attention to the pictures once more.

The first victim, Ava King, was a woman in her mid-30s with shoulder-length chestnut hair framing her oval face and piercing green eyes. Originally from Maine, Ava had been working as a freelance travel journalist when she visited Louisiana to document the unique wildlife and culture of the swamps for an upcoming article. The day before she was killed, Ava had interviewed a local family about their experiences living in such a remote area. None of the members of that family, however, knew anything about Ava's plans for the following day.

Jacob Ramirez, the second victim, had dark skin and a mop of curly black hair atop his head. He was a geologist from Arizona who worked for an environmental conservation organization specializing in wetlands preservation. Jacob had traveled to Louisiana to conduct research on the geological and ecological aspects of the swamplands. He had spent weeks collecting soil samples and mapping the region's waterways before he was found dead, his body half-submerged in murky swamp waters.

Patrick Sharma, the third victim, was a tall, lanky man in his early 40s with a scruffy beard and piercing blue eyes that spoke of a life lived in solitude. Born and raised in the Louisiana swamps, Patrick had made a modest living trapping and fishing before turning up floating on a sea of algae.

And then, of course, there was Jennifer Easton.

"Four victims," Peyton said, raising her voice to be heard about the hum of the fans. "All seemingly unrelated, but there has to be something connecting them."

"Let's see," Sean said, tapping his finger on his chin thoughtfully. "Three of the victims were here for work, but the fourth – Patrick – lived here. So that rules out the idea that our killer is just targeting tourists."

"Not many similarities in their personal lives, either," Peyton said. "Ava was single and didn't have any children, while Jennifer was married but had no kids. Jacob was divorced but had two sons who lived with their mother in Arizona. Patrick, as far as we know, never married or had any children."

"Ava was something of a social butterfly, while Patrick was definitely a loner. No connection there, either. And the times are all over the place—Ava was murdered three weeks ago, the sixth of the month; Jacob was murdered on the eighth; Patrick was murdered on the nineteenth, about a week ago; and then Jennifer…" He paused. "Well, she was probably murdered in the past few days. We'll have to wait for the coroner to give us a clearer idea on that."

Peyton chewed on her lower lip, considering these facts. "There's no obvious link between any of them. Maybe if we dig deeper into their backgrounds, though, we'll find something that ties them together."

"Let's start by looking into their online presence and see if any patterns emerge," Sean said. "Who knows? Maybe the killer knew all of them. We could get lucky."

Peyton didn't believe in luck, but she opened her laptop and looked up Jacob Ramirez's social media profile, nonetheless. As she scrolled through his posts, she noticed that most of them were related to wetlands preservation, and he often shared articles about local efforts to save the fragile ecosystem. Her eyes narrowed as she spotted a recurring commenter on many of his posts, a handle by the name of "BogLover93."

"Sean," Peyton called. "Come have a look at this."

Sean rolled over to her and leaned in to study the screen. "BogLover93?" He snorted lightly, shaking his head. "Some people come up with the strangest usernames."

Throwing him a dry look, Peyton clicked onto BogLover93's profile. It was private but the bio read: "Born and raised in the swamps of Louisiana. The bog is my church, my home. Lover of all creatures living and dead."

"A bit morbid," Sean commented, grimacing slightly.

Peyton nodded distractedly before returning to Jacob's posts to find the comments left by BogLover93. They varied from supportive messages about conservation to angry rants against corporations destroying the wetland ecosystem.

"I'm going to see if BogLover93 has interacted with our other victims," Peyton said, already typing away rapidly.

Ava had a blog documenting her travels. A quick search revealed that she had written about the environmental challenges facing Louisiana swamps, with comments from BogLover93 applauding her efforts and providing more local insights. Patrick Sharma didn't have much of a digital footprint, but an old forum post about fishing in the swamp had a reply from BogLover93, advising him on the best spots to catch native species. Jennifer Easton had a Twitter account mostly used for her job as a climate change activist; among the hundreds of likes and retweets, Peyton found interactions with BogLover93.

"He's interacted with all of them," Peyton said, glancing at Sean. "BogLover93 could be our connection."

"Or just an environmental enthusiast," Sean countered, though he looked intrigued. "Let's not get ahead of ourselves. We need to find out who he is first."

"Right," Peyton said, turning back to her laptop. She quickly keyed into the database, setting up a search for the username. "I'll see if we can get some more information on him."

The two rangers fell silent as the computer whirred quietly, processing the inquiry. The office hummed around them, the steady murmur of activity providing a soothing backdrop to their tense investigation. As Peyton worked at tracking BogLover93, Sean leaned back in his chair, arms folded across his chest as he studied the victims' photos on the wall.

Suddenly, Peyton's fingers stilled on her keyboard. "I think I've got something," she said. "I traced the IP address for BogLover93's comments."

"And?" Sean asked, leaning forward in anticipation.

"It's coming from a place called Lagniappe Lodge," Peyton said as she zoomed into the satellite map. "It's in the heart of the swamp."

Sean frowned, his gaze sliding to Ava King's picture. "Wasn't that where Ava King stayed during her visit here?"

Peyton nodded as she scrolled through Ava's travel blog again. "Yes. She mentioned it here in one of her posts." She looked over at Sean, an unspoken question hanging between them.

"Looks like we're taking a trip to the swamp," Sean said.

CHAPTER TEN

"They couldn't have made it any creepier if they'd tried," Peyton said.

Lagniappe Lodge was a ramshackle structure straight out of a Southern Gothic novel—creaky wooden planks, an abundance of Spanish moss hanging from the roof edges, and a weathered sign barely hanging by a rusted chain.

They had come prepared for whatever they might find, equipping themselves with chest waders, headlamps, life vests, and waterproof bags, all of which Wilder had been kind enough to let them borrow. They knew the unpredictable nature of swampland; better to be over-prepared than under.

As Peyton and Sean approached the lodge's front porch, an elderly woman appeared in the doorway. Her eyes were sunken but sharp as she surveyed them and their garb. "

"Y'all didn't come to bird-watch, did ya?" she croaked, leaning on her cane for support. Her clothes were old-fashioned, and her hair, wild and unkempt, was a nest of silver curls.

Peyton shook her head, offering a polite smile. "Ma'am, we're here on official business. We're investigating some recent incidents and we believe a person who may have information is staying at this lodge." Peyton held out her ID for the woman to see.

The woman squinted at the badge before chuckling dryly. "Well, ain't that something? Never had lawmen come around these parts in all my years."

Sean stepped forward. "We're hoping you might be able to help us. Do you know anyone who goes by the username 'BogLover93'?"

"Depends. What's a username?"

Peyton and Sean exchanged a glance before Peyton tried to explain. "It's a digital name used on the internet, ma'am. For websites, social media, forums, emails...that sort of thing."

The elderly woman frowned at her words, shaking her head slightly. "Don't know about any of that. We don't get much use for the internet out here," she said, her voice raspy from years of smoking. "Most folks around here are just swamp folk—living off the land, not stuck on their computers all day." There was a faint note of disdain in her tone.

"Well," Sean said, leaning against the porch railing. "This person we're looking for—they seem to be quite concerned with the local swamp. They're very invested in conservation efforts, and they interact with people who have the same interests."

The woman seemed to consider this for a moment before she nodded slowly. "That sounds like Drew," she said after a moment.

"Drew?" Peyton repeated, pulling out a notebook to jot down the name.

"Yes," the woman confirmed. "Drew Lejeune. He's my great-nephew. Boy's got a mind full of critters and marshland plants. Always going on about saving our swamps."

"Can we speak with him?" Sean asked.

"Drew ain't here right now," she replied, her gaze slowly moving to the vast expanse of swamp beyond the reach of the lodge. "He's gone into the bog. Been gone since yesterday."

"Yesterday?" Peyton echoed, her brows furrowed in concern. "Isn't that unusual?"

"Nonsense," the woman brushed off with a wave of her gnarled hand. "Ain't nothing unusual about Drew spending a night in the swamp. He's more at home there than here."

"We'd really like to talk to him as soon as possible. Can you tell us where he might be? We can go to him instead."

The woman raised a skeptical eyebrow. "You got a boat?"

Peyton faltered. "No, not at the moment."

"Well, unless you fancy swimming, you ain't gonna reach him. Better wait here and let him come to you."

Sean eyed her thoughtfully for a moment. "In the meantime, ma'am, if you don't mind, we'd like to look around his room."

The elderly woman paused at that, her sharp eyes studying them for a moment before she nodded grudgingly. "Why? He in some kind of trouble?"

"We're just trying to understand a few things, ma'am," Sean reassured her. "Drew isn't under any suspicion."

Something about Sean's soft-spoken reassurance seemed to put her at ease. She creaked open the screen door farther and beckoned for them to follow her inside.

The interior of the lodge was dim and spacious, filled with an array of mismatched furniture. As the woman led them through a narrow hallway, Peyton noticed photos lining the walls: pictures of Drew, she guessed, throughout various stages of his life.

The room the woman ushered them into was small and musty, with cracked windows looking out onto the swamp. An old bed sat against one wall, its coverlet worn thin over time, while a dusty desk piled high with books and papers occupied another corner.

Sean and Peyton began sifting through the clutter as the woman excused herself, settling in a nearby rocking chair on the porch. The room felt untouched, as if frozen in a bygone era when Drew was still around. There were books on amphibians, birds, flora and fauna, each showing signs of heavy use.

But it was Peyton who found what they were looking for—in between pages of a hefty book on marsh ecology lay printed screenshots of interactions with Jennifer Easton on social media. Blog posts from Ava King were meticulously highlighted for some reason.

"Sean, look at this." Peyton held out the damning evidence, her gloved hand careful not to smudge the ink. Sean glanced over her shoulder, his brows lifting in surprise.

"Well, well," he mused. "Isn't that something? Our swamp-loving friend is quite the stalker."

There was another detail that caught Peyton's attention. The comments by BogLover93 weren't just random interactions; they were advancements. Compliments on Ava's beauty and intelligence—strategic compliments designed to build trust and endearment.

"He was grooming her," Peyton murmured, her gut twisting with a sickening realization. "He was building a relationship with her online under the pretense of conservation."

Sean grimaced. "And she walked right into it, thinking she'd found a kindred spirit who cared about the same things she did."

They continued their search, uncovering more evidence of Drew's obsession with Ava King. There were notes scribbled on scraps of paper—disjointed thoughts and ideas that hinted at intentions deeper than mere admiration.

Just then, the sound of an airboat motor cut through the murky stillness that surrounded Lagniappe Lodge. Peyton and Sean exchanged a look, their hands simultaneously reaching for their guns.

"Sounds like Drew's back," came the woman's voice from the porch. "You best finish up."

The agents hastily gathered up the papers, tucking them into protective bags before moving to exit the room. As they emerged onto the porch, a battered airboat was pulling up to the dock. A lanky figure was hunched over the controls, a wide-brimmed hat obscuring his features.

"Drew," called the elderly woman. "You've got visitors."

The figure straightened, pushing back his hat to reveal a young man who couldn't have been more than twenty-five. His face was smudged with dirt, and his hair was tousled from the wind, but his eyes were bright and intelligent.

"Aunt Mabel," he called back in surprise. "Who are they?"

"Manners, boy," Aunt Mabel chastised gently. She turned to Peyton and Sean, jerking her head toward Drew. "Go on and talk to him. Drew ain't one for formalities."

Peyton stepped forward first, pulling out her badge once again. "Mr. Lejeune," she began formally, her voice steady despite her racing heart. "I'm Ranger Peyton Risk, with the National Park Service," she said and gestured to Sean, who was pulling out his own badge. "This is my partner, Ranger Sean O'Malley."

Drew's expression changed from surprise to curiosity. "Rangers? What are you doing here?" he asked, tying up the boat before jumping on the dock.

"We'd like to speak with you about a certain online persona known as BogLover93," Peyton stated.

A flicker of recognition passed across Drew's features but quickly vanished. "What about it?" he asked, feigning indifference.

Sean took over then, building upon Peyton's introduction. "We believe this persona may have information relating to an ongoing investigation. We understand that you're heavily involved in conservation efforts in this area, and we're hoping you could help us."

He paused for a moment, allowing Drew to digest the information. The young man looked between the two rangers, his confusion evident in his gaze.

"I don't understand how that's connected to me," Drew replied evasively. "I do what I can for the swamp, sure. But my actions don't involve any criminal activity."

"No one said they did, son," Sean responded, backing off slightly. "It's just that this BogLover93—well, whoever created that persona seems to be connected to four people who've mysteriously wound up dead in these swamps in the past month."

Drew paled considerably at this revelation, his swamp-weathered face turning a shade of ghost-white. "Dead?" he echoed, his voice trembling.

"Yes," Peyton confirmed gravely. "In tragic circumstances. All four, we believe, were murdered."

"Their names were Jennifer Easton, Ava King, Jacob Ramirez, and Patrick Sharma," Sean added, watching Drew's face closely for any flicker of recognition.

Drew's gaze dropped to the wooden planks beneath his feet. "I don't recognize those names," he muttered almost to himself.

"You sure about that?" Peyton pressed. She pulled out the screenshots and notes they'd found in Drew's room and presented them to him. "We found these in your room."

For a moment, there was only a deafening silence as Drew scanned over the pieces of damning evidence laid bare before him.

Peyton decided to push further. "You've been having online conversations with Ava King under the pseudonym BogLover93."

"What?" Drew's gaze snapped up to meet hers, his eyes wide with shock. "No...no, I didn't—I mean, I did talk to her but—"

"We know everything, Drew," Sean cut him off sternly. "Stop lying."

"I'm not—" Drew began, but his mouth snapped shut as his gaze fell on the printed screenshots again. Slowly, he sank onto one of the dock's benches, his face a mix of shock and disbelief.

"I didn't mean to..." His voice trailed off, the words barely a whisper against the swamp's persistent hum.

"Didn't mean to what?" Peyton asked sharply, her patience wearing thin. "Didn't mean to charm her? Didn't mean to lure her into your world? Or didn't mean to kill her?"

The accusation hung heavy in the air. Drew looked between Peyton and Sean, his gaze filled with horror. "No...no..." he stuttered. "I didn't kill anyone."

Aunt Mabel, who had been silent till now, spoke up from the porch. "Drew wouldn't hurt a fly," she said. "He's a good boy."

"Good people do bad things all the time," Sean said.

The discordant silence stretched for an agonizing moment before Drew finally spoke again, his voice raspy. "Ask me whatever you want...I'll cooperate completely," he said. "But I swear I didn't murder anyone."

Peyton and Sean exchanged glances before Peyton pulled out a small notebook from her pocket. "Tell us about your relationship with Ava, then," she said. She knew Ava had stayed at this very lodge—Ava had mentioned it on her travel blog. The question was, would Drew own up to it or lie about it?

Drew swallowed hard, his wide eyes flicking from Peyton to Sean and then back again. "We met online...on a conservation forum," he began, his voice shaky. "We started talking...she said she was coming down for a visit, wanted some tips on what to see."

"Did she stay here?" Peyton probed, her gaze steady on Drew's nervous face.

He hesitated for a moment before nodding reluctantly. "Yes, she did."

"And during her stay here?"

"We talked a lot about the swamp, its beauty…" Drew stuttered out before trailing off, glancing at Aunt Mabel.

"So you spent time with her?" Sean cut in swiftly. His dark eyes were unwavering on Drew's uneasy face.

"Only a little," he replied hastily. "I showed her around some parts of the swamp. That's all."

The more Peyton studied this young man, the more she doubted he was capable of strangling to death four innocent people. He seemed too...simple. That was what her gut told her, anyway. They were still a long way from proving his innocence, however. The only one of the four victims he was closely tied to was Ava, so if they could prove he hadn't killed Ava, then perhaps they could rule him out for the others as well.

"So you're saying that after you showed her around, that was the end of your interaction with Ava?" Peyton pressed.

Drew nodded, a mixture of fear and earnestness in his eyes. "Yes, I swear it."

"Any idea who would want to harm her?" Sean asked, scrutinizing Drew's face for any hint of deception.

"I...I don't know," Drew stuttered, his face paling further under their relentless questioning. "She was a nice girl, passionate about preserving nature...I can't think of anyone who'd want to hurt her."

Peyton felt a pang of sympathy for Drew. He was clearly in over his head. But if he was innocent, he was their best lead to finding the real killer.

"After she left," Peyton said, "did Ava say anything about where she was going or what she was doing?"

Drew shook his head. "No, she didn't. She just thanked me for my help and went on her way," he replied, his confusion clear in his voice.

"I didn't hear from her again. I...I didn't know something had happened to her until you told me."

"Did you ever have contact with her after that?" Peyton asked.

Again, Drew shook his head. "No," he protested weakly. "I swear, I didn't see or talk to her after that."

Peyton took a few steps forward, looking into the murky depths of the swamp. "We'll need to verify all this information," she called back over her shoulder. "Can you provide any proof of your whereabouts last Friday?"

Drew looked shell-shocked as he nodded. "I...yes," he stuttered. "I always carry my GPS tracker when I'm out in the swamp...for safety." He shrugged, looking helpless as he added, "It records everywhere I've been."

That perked Sean's interest. "Can we see it?"

Drew hesitated for a moment before getting up and disappearing into the lodge. Seconds passed. Peyton stiffened, wondering if they'd just made a terrible mistake. Was Drew making his escape while they sat here, waiting like idiots?

Just when Peyton was thinking of going after Drew, he returned holding a small device in his trembling hands. "It's...it's right here," he said, presenting it to Sean.

Sean took the GPS tracker, giving Drew a hard look before turning his attention to the small device. He began scrolling through the stored data as Peyton watched Drew closely. The young man looked like he was on the verge of a breakdown, and Peyton couldn't help but feel a pang of sympathy for him—assuming he was innocent, of course.

"Well," Sean finally said after a few moments, his voice tight. "Seems you were deep in the swamp all last Friday and through most of Saturday." He sighed and handed the GPS back to Drew. "We appreciate your time, Mr. Lejeune."

"We'll be in touch," Peyton added, standing up and extending a hand for Drew to shake. Drew merely nodded, accepting her handshake with a weak grip.

As they left the lodge, Peyton felt her heart sinking like a stone dropped in deep water. If Drew wasn't the killer...then who was?

CHAPTER ELEVEN

"We have to keep digging," Peyton said, wearily pulling off her boots. "Even if we have to speak with every suspicious character any of the victims have ever run into, we have to do what we can. There's no alternative."

They were back in the precinct, back with the droning fans and the cloistered heat. All they had to show for their work was sweat, mud, and lost time.

"There's just one problem," Sean said, scratching at a mosquito bite on his arm. "If our killer is targeting a new victim – and I know that's a big if – then that person might not have much time left."

Peyton sighed. She'd been thinking the same thing. Still, the only thing they could do was to follow the best leads they had. At the end of the day, that was all they could control.

"Are you hungry?" Sean said suddenly. "It's almost two o'clock in the afternoon, and we've barely eaten anything all day."

With a laugh, Peyton leaned back against her chair with an exaggerated groan. "Never thought I'd be so happy to hear you talk about food, Sean."

He grinned at her before standing up, stretching his tall frame. "I'll go grab us something from the food truck outside."

As Sean left the room, Peyton turned back to her computer, opening up the case file again. She went through their notes, scrutinizing each detail as if she were searching for a hidden message. Hal Reddish's words about Jennifer Easton wanting to visit a 'haunted island' came back to her.

I wonder if Jennifer ever made it there, she thought. *I wonder if any of the victims did.*

Curious, Peyton started searching the victims' social media profiles for any posts about islands. On Jacob Ramirez's profile, buried beneath pictures of geological formations and posts about environmental conservation efforts, she discovered a post Jacob had written about planning a trip to a 'haunted island' in Louisiana.

Just then, Sean returned with two styrofoam cartons filled with steaming food. "Get it while it's hot," he said.

"Look at this," Peyton said, gesturing for Sean to come closer. She pointed at Jacob's post about the haunted island. "Jacob mentioned visiting a haunted island in Louisiana. And earlier, Reddish told us Jennifer had plans to visit the same place. Could that be a coincidence?"

Sean frowned as he studied the screen. "Not likely," he said slowly.

Just then, there came a knock at the door. Officer Wilder poked his head into the room, his burly frame barely fitting through the doorway. He wiped the sweat from his eyes with the back of his hand, leaving a faint trace of grime in its wake, then stopped abruptly when he saw their takeout containers.

"Ah," he said.

"What is it?" Sean asked.

"I was just about to say I'm sending one of the boys on a lunch run," he said, his voice tinged with the distinctive drawl of the bayou. "Looks like y'all don't need any help, though."

Sean smiled. "Just picked it up from the food truck."

"Well, be careful about them spices. Old Joe don't spare any." Wilder began to turn away. Before he could get far, however, Peyton called him back.

"Officer Wilder," she said. "Have you ever heard of a haunted island nearby?"

At first, Wilder seemed to think Peyton was making a joke. His thick eyebrows furrowed as his mouth twisted into a half-smirk, half-frown. But as he looked into her unwavering eyes, he seemed to realize she was deadly serious.

"Uh, well," he began hesitantly, scratching at the jagged scar that marred his left cheek. "There is one island 'round here folks talk about sometimes. Got a real creepy history, if you believe the stories."

Peyton leaned forward, her heart pounding in her chest. This could be the connection they were searching for, the missing piece of the puzzle. "What's special about the island?" she asked.

"From what I've heard," Wilder said, glancing around as though he expected someone to materialize out of thin air and eavesdrop on their conversation, "the island was used for some...occultic practices back in the day. There's all sorts of disturbing rumors 'bout the place."

Peyton exchanged a significant glance with Sean, who nodded almost imperceptibly. The haunted island had to be connected to their victims somehow. They just needed to figure out how it fit into the bigger picture.

"Where is this island?" Peyton asked.

Wilder shifted uncomfortably, his burly frame tense beneath his police uniform. He glanced away from Peyton, as if afraid to meet her gaze. "Folks 'round here tend to avoid that place," he said, his thick Southern accent heavy with unease. "I ain't superstitious, mind you, but I am a religious man. I don't like messin' with things I don't understand."

Sean leaned forward, resting his elbows on the desk. His eyes were sharp and calculating. "Can you take us there, Officer Wilder? You don't even have to step foot on the island."

"Sorry, I can't," Wilder replied, his voice tight. "Got my hands full with other duties."

"Could one of the other officers take us?" Peyton asked, undeterred.

Wilder shook his head, a pained expression crossing his scarred face. "You can ask, but I doubt you'll find any takers. Like I said, people avoid that place for good reason."

As frustration bubbled within her, an idea struck Peyton. She recalled the strange character they had encountered earlier—Wilder's brother-in-law, Chip. He seemed like the type who might be willing to venture where others wouldn't. "What about Chip?" she suggested, watching Wilder closely for his reaction.

"Chip?" Wilder frowned, clearly taken aback by the suggestion. He hesitated, his fingers drumming against the doorframe as he considered the possibility. "You know, now that you mention it, he might be just crazy enough to take you up on the offer." He sighed. "That doesn't mean it's a good idea, though."

"We can handle ourselves," Peyton said.

"Maybe you can. You see, the thing is, Chip's spent all his life in these swamps, so he's comfortable with a lot of its dangers. But you two?" He shook his head, his expression grim. "You don't stand a chance. Mark my words: If you go out there, that swamp will swallow you whole—and you may never be seen or heard from again."

CHAPTER TWELVE

Wilder's warning echoed in Peyton's ears as the airboat sped through the murky swamp waters, its powerful engine propelling them forward. Peyton gripped the side of the boat tightly, her knuckles white from the pressure as Chip maneuvered the vessel with surprising ease. Her stomach churned with each sharp turn, and she silently prayed that their journey would be worth the discomfort.

The scenery passing by was a hauntingly beautiful blend of darkness and light. Spanish moss draped over the gnarled branches of ancient cypress trees like a ghostly veil, while sunlight filtered through the dense canopy overhead, casting dappled shadows on the water's surface. All around them, the swamp teemed with life: frogs croaked from the safety of floating logs, snakes slithered stealthily through the undergrowth, and the occasional splash signaled the retreat of an alligator disturbed by the airboat's approach.

As they traveled deeper into the swampland, Peyton found herself studying Chip more closely. If Jennifer had been searching for someone to guide her through the swamps, who better than a local tour guide like Chip? Was it possible Chip was involved somehow?

"Y'all were askin' about that haunted island," Chip said suddenly, breaking the silence that had settled between them. "Used to be called Île des Serpents Morts—Island of the Dead Snakes. Had a real bad reputation back in the day. Folks said it was used for occult practices and such."

Peyton shivered involuntarily at the mention of dead snakes. She could handle most creatures, but there was something particularly unsettling about serpents.

"Rumor has it," Chip continued, "that when the police finally raided the place, they found dozens of dead snakes hangin' from the trees. Just like a scene outta hell."

"If that's the case," Sean said, "then why aren't you worried about going out to this island? Nobody else seemed interested."

Chip's eyes flicked over to Sean, a sardonic grin playing at the corners of his mouth. "Well, truth be told, I'm not much for superstitions. Besides, I've had my fair share of close calls in life

60

already."

"Close calls?" Peyton asked.

"Yep." Chip nodded, steering the airboat around a grove of gnarled roots. "When I was just a kid, maybe twelve or so, I got caught up in a bad accident out here in the swamps. Was tryna catch some gators when my hand slipped, and wouldn't you know it," he paused, raising his right hand for them to see, "lost these three fingers clean off."

Peyton winced as she examined the mangled appendage.

"Ever since then," Chip continued, his voice taking on a more somber tone, "I've felt like my fate was pretty much out of my hands. When it's my time to go, I'll go. Nothing I can do about it, so why worry?"

"Sounds fatalistic," Sean remarked, his expression unreadable.

"Maybe it is," Chip acknowledged with a shrug. "But I've made my peace with the world. Ain't nothing left to do but ride it out, see what happens next."

Just then, the airboat glided to a stop, its murky waters lapping gently against a tree-lined shore. Peyton's eyes widened as she took in the expanse of land before them. The island was bigger than she had expected, its dense foliage and gnarled trees giving it an eerie, otherworldly atmosphere.

"Wow," she muttered, unable to find any other words to describe the strange beauty of the place.

Chip parked the boat but didn't make any move to get out. Sean furrowed his brow and asked, "Aren't you coming with us?"

"Nah," Chip replied, shaking his head. "I'll stay here with the boat."

Sean raised an eyebrow. "I thought you said your fate was out of your hands."

"True," Chip admitted, his gaze focused on the distance, "but I ain't suicidal, either."

Peyton frowned, unsure what to make of this comment. They couldn't exactly make Chip go ashore against his will, however, so Peyton shrugged and climbed out of the boat, followed by Sean.

Stepping onto the island, Peyton felt the damp earth squelch beneath her boots. The air was heavy with humidity, and the scent of rotting vegetation filled her nostrils. Moss-draped cypress trees loomed overhead, their knotted roots snaking through the muddy ground. Shafts of sunlight struggled to penetrate the thick canopy, casting the island in a perpetual twilight.

"Man, this place is so different from Montana," Sean remarked, swatting at a mosquito that buzzed near his ear. "I don't think I'll ever get used to these swamps."

"Me neither," Peyton said, her eyes darting around their surroundings. She had the uncomfortable sensation she was being watched.

As they walked, the undergrowth grew denser, and the sounds of the outside world faded away until all that remained was the steady rhythm of their footsteps and the occasional rustle of leaves overhead. Soon, the boat was lost from sight, swallowed by the verdant landscape.

Peyton's eyes were drawn to a massive cypress in the center of the island, its gnarled roots spreading out like the tentacles of some ancient leviathan. The bark was rough and weathered, its deep grooves forming intricate patterns that seemed to tell the story of countless storms and battles it had faced throughout the centuries. Thick branches reached toward the sky as if longing to touch the clouds above.

As she stepped closer, Peyton noticed the skeletons of a few small animals hanging from the branches, their tiny bones bleached white by the sun. She wondered what sort of creatures they had been, and how they had ended up here—dangling in the shadows of this ancient sentinel. She shuddered.

That didn't happen by accident, she thought.

"Check it out," Sean said, his voice jolting her from her reverie. He was pointing at something on the ground nearby, a mixture of curiosity and concern etched across his angular face. "You need to see this."

Reluctantly tearing her gaze away from the tree, Peyton joined Sean at the edge of a small clearing. Her eyes widened as she took in the scene before her. A hastily-dug fire pit lay at the center of the clearing, its edges blackened from recent use. Empty beer cans and other debris littered the ground around it, creating a stark contrast to the eerie beauty of the cypress tree just a few yards away.

"Looks like someone had a party here," Sean remarked, his eyes narrowing as he surveyed the area. "Not exactly an ideal spot for a celebration, if you ask me."

Peyton nodded, thinking. Who would choose such a place for a gathering? And more importantly, could this have something to do with Jennifer's disappearance? Had she been here?

Peyton's gaze swept over the ground near the fire pit, her eyes narrowing as they caught sight of a series of footprints partially obscured in the mud. She crouched down and examined them more closely, her heart pounding with anticipation.

Peyton pulled out her phone, scrolling through the images stored within until she found what she was looking for—a photograph of Jennifer's sneakers, taken during the course of their investigation. She held it up next to the footprints.

"It's a match," Peyton said, turning to see Sean looming beside her, his eyebrows pinched together. "Whatever happened here...there's no question Jennifer Easton was on this island."

"The question is," he said, "who was on the island with her? And what did they do to her?"

CHAPTER THIRTEEN

High above, concealed among the twisted branches of the ancient cypress tree, the man seethed with fury as he watched the two NPS officers violate his sacred space. His fingers dug into the bark, leaving crescent-shaped marks in the weathered surface. He longed to leap down and strangle them with his bare hands, end their trespassing once and for all.

"Damn it," the man muttered under his breath, watching the two officers examine the footprints in the mud nearby. He knew they would realize Jennifer had been here, and now their search for her would intensify. With each passing second, his fury grew. How dare they intrude on this sacred place.

The man's heart hammered as he watched them. How could they not understand the importance of this place? For generations, people had known of its sacred nature, and that knowledge had been passed down through whispered stories and late-night tales. It was here that sacrifices had been made, offerings given to appease the unseen forces that lurked in the shadows of the swamp.

He remembered the first time he had come to this place, led by the whispers of his ancestors. As he stood among the twisted roots and gnarled branches, he felt the weight of their expectations, the burden of their legacy pressing down on him. He knew it was his duty to continue their work, to protect the sanctity of this land from those who would defile it.

The man's gaze settled on the woman, her face lit up with grim determination. She looked so out of place amidst the ancient trees and murky waters, a stranger in a land that didn't want her. A land that would fight back if it had to.

His hands gripped tighter around the tree branch he was perched on, his fingers digging into the rough bark. Each breath he took was filled with the heady scent of decaying leaves and damp earth, the signature perfume of the swamp. It comforted him.

He knew the island like the back of his hand—every inch of ground, every gnarled root, every shadowy corner. He knew how to navigate it in complete darkness, how to move silently through the underbrush without leaving a trace of his presence behind.

And he knew its secrets, secrets he'd kill to protect if necessary. The blood of those who had defiled his sacred space still clung to his hands, a gruesome testament to his fierce resolve.

"Leave," he whispered into the wind, his voice barely above a sigh. "Before you force my hand."

But the two figures were engrossed in their investigation, oblivious to the deadly threat lurking overhead. They moved around the clearing like they owned it, their voices as violating in this space as the drone of an engine or the rhythm of an electric guitar.

The man watched from his perch in the tree as the two figures disappeared deeper into the swamp, swallowed up by the gnarled roots and thick foliage. Every muscle in his body tensed, itching to pursue them, to end their intrusion. But he knew he needed to be cautious. Taking a deep breath, he began his descent.

The ancient cypress tree's bark was rough beneath his fingertips, its horizontal branches offering sturdy footholds for his booted feet. Moss hung like tattered curtains from the limbs, concealing him from view. The tree had been here for centuries, its massive trunk bearing witness to generations of rituals and sacrifices that had taken place in this sacred grove.

"Leaving you is always hard, old friend," he whispered to the tree, feeling an odd sense of camaraderie with the steadfast sentinel. "But I have work to do."

He moved with the grace of a predator, limb by limb, until his boots met the damp earth below. Decaying leaves and mulch muffled his footsteps as he followed the officers' path, staying low and using the tangled undergrowth to his advantage.

As he crept through the swamp, the man's mind swirled with images of the past. He remembered the faces of those who had come before him, the proud lineage of guardians who had protected this land. They had passed down their knowledge, their reverence for the power that pulsed beneath the waterlogged soil. And now, it was his responsibility to continue their legacy.

Concealed in the shadows, the man's hand slipped into his pocket, fingertips brushing against the cold steel of his knife. It was a simple weapon, but deadly in the right hands. The blade was long and slender, its edge honed to razor-sharpness. The handle, carved from the bone of a past sacrifice, fit comfortably in his grip. It wasn't his preferred method of execution, but under the circumstances, it was probably the most practical.

With his heart singing a furious rhythm in his chest, the man slipped deeper into the swamp, each step taking him closer to the intruders. He could hear their voices now, clearer than before, their words slicing through the silence of the sacred grove like a jagged blade.

"I can see why nobody wanted to come out here," the woman said. "This place sure is creepy."

The man's lips twisted into a cruel smile at their discomfort. They were right to feel uneasy. This was not their realm, not their sanctuary.

The memory of Jennifer Easton flickered in his mind. A stubborn girl with a fiery spirit. She'd been a challenge, that one, but he'd handled her—just as he would deal with these two pests.

Moving with the stealth and precision of a hunting cat, the man drew nearer, keeping himself concealed behind the thick foliage. Sweat trickled down his brow as he carefully navigated the twisted roots and muddy ground underfoot. He tightened his grip on the knife, anticipation flaring within him.

He slipped behind a tree trunk, keeping his head low as he peeked back around.

Why do they persist? he thought, rage simmering just below the surface. *This island is mine, my sanctuary, and they dare to defile it with their presence. They can't understand what this place means—or what I'll do to protect it.*

Soon, however, they would know. Soon they would understand.

I'll just have to find a way to separate them, pick one of them off. Then the other will be easy.

He smiled, amused by this plan.

His gaze flitted back to the two officers again, studying them intently. The woman walked with a certain toughness, her eyes scanning the environment vigilantly; she was careful, alert. The man, on the other hand, seemed more relaxed, less focused. Then again, he was bigger and might very well put up more of a fight.

Decisions, decisions.

The man crept stealthily behind the cover of the trees, his eyes never leaving his prey. The pair came to a stop near a small pool of murky water. He heard them converse about something inaudible from his distance. He watched as they bent down near the water's edge, where they seemed to find something interesting.

Taking advantage of their brief distraction, he moved closer, staying low to the ground. His every movement was cautious and calculated. His heart pounded in his chest with wild exhilaration, but he remained calm and focused.

As he neared them, he slipped his hand into his pocket and wrapped his fingers around the cool handle of the knife once more. Its familiar touch sent shivers up his spine.

Looks like your little investigation's about to end, he thought.

CHAPTER FOURTEEN

"Quite a party, indeed," Peyton said as she and Sean stepped into the small clearing, which was littered with empty beer bottles. Peyton recalled what the coroner had said about Jennifer Easton being heavily intoxicated when she was killed.

Had Jennifer come here and continued drinking after her time at the bar? Had she, after parting ways with Hal Reddish, found someone else to take her here, partied for a while, and then been murdered either by someone with her or someone she'd encountered out here in the wilderness?

And what of her original plan to scout the area for tourism opportunities for her marketing consultancy firm? Wasn't that Jennifer's reason for being in Louisiana in the first place?

"I don't get it," Peyton said. "Did Jennifer have a drinking problem we don't know about? Or was she just trying to mingle with the locals, and she went a little too far?"

"Much too far, I'd say," Sean answered, nudging a bottle with his boot. "Then again, when in Rome..."

"This is about the furthest thing from Rome I can imagine," Peyton replied.

As Peyton walked the perimeter of the clearing, a shiver ran down her spine. She felt watched, studied. She glanced around, but all she could see were dark trees standing prim and silent; their shadows danced ominously as the wind whipped through the gnarled branches.

"Let's hurry this up," she suggested. "I don't like this place."

"Don't move."

Peyton turned, puzzled by the tone of Sean's voice. He was a short distance away, his gaze fixed on something to Peyton's left. She looked that way and saw, camouflaged against the muddy ground, a long snake. It was coiled tightly, its forked tongue darting out as it tested the air around it. It was resting its head on a flat stone, a hypnotic pattern painted across its scales—vibrant greens and yellows melding flawlessly with the surrounding foliage.

"It's a cottonmouth," Sean said, his eyes not leaving the snake. "Venomous."

Peyton swallowed hard, forcing herself to stay calm. She knew better than to make any sudden movements that might provoke the creature.

"Just stay where you are," Sean said in a calm voice. "Don't move." Without taking his eyes off the snake, Sean bent and picked up a fallen branch. The end of the branch forked, making a *v*.

"What are you going to do?" Peyton asked, her mouth suddenly dry.

"I'm going to pin its head so you can move away safely."

"Have you done this before?"

"Lots of times. Just trust me."

He is *a wilderness survival expert,* Peyton thought. *That's got to count for something.*

As Sean slowly approached the snake, Peyton remained still, her breath stuck in her throat. She watched as Sean slowly lowered the forked part of the branch over the snake's head. The cottonmouth hissed, instantly aware of the threat.

Sean didn't flinch. He moved quickly, pinning the snake's head to the ground with the branch. It writhed and squirmed beneath the pressure, its hissing intensifying.

"Okay," Sean said in a low voice, "I want you to back away slowly."

Peyton nodded, not trusting herself to speak. She took slow, deliberate steps backward, her eyes on Sean and the thrashing snake all the while. When she had put enough distance between herself and the cottonmouth, Sean released the pressure on his improvised tool.

The snake slithered away with incredible speed, disappearing into the underbrush. Sean let out a sigh of relief as he turned toward Peyton.

"You okay?" he asked, his tone softer now.

"Yeah," Peyton answered, letting out a shaky breath she hadn't realized she was holding. "Thanks."

They stood for a moment longer in tense silence. As Peyton's heartbeat calmed down, she found herself tremendously grateful for Sean's swift action. She thought about his confidence, his readiness to intervene.

"It could've bitten you," she said. "You didn't have to put yourself in harm's way like that."

He grinned. "That's why I used a long stick." Then his smile faded, and he grew more serious. "It's what we do—we watch each other's backs. I know you'd do the same for me."

Something in his voice made her look at him. He was staring at her with an intensity that made her heart flutter. But before she could respond, Sean was back to business, clearing his throat and tossing the stick aside.

"Let's get back to it, shall we?" he said, breaking the moment. "We've still got a lot of ground to cover."

Peyton nodded, forcing herself to recenter. They were here for a reason—not to flirt or get bitten by snakes, but to solve a murder. She took a deep breath and followed Sean as he left the clearing along a narrow path.

There was an awkward silence between them as they resumed their search. The incident with the snake had somehow shifted the dynamic between her and Sean. It wasn't their first life-or-death situation together, but there was something about his protective instinct that felt deeply personal this time around.

Would he have responded that quickly with just anyone? Peyton wondered.

She was still thinking about this when Sean pulled up abruptly.

"What is it?" Peyton asked.

"Look," he said, pointing. Peyton joined him and saw that they were back at the fire pit. They'd gone in a circle.

"I'm not sure we're going to have much luck exploring this island on our own," Sean said. "It's too dense to go off the path."

"We need more manpower," Peyton said, "locals who know this terrain."

"And machetes, too. Definitely machetes."

Peyton didn't argue. "Let's head back to the boat, then," she said, trying not to feel discouraged. They had, after all, learned something very valuable: They now knew that Jennifer Easton had been here on this island. The question was, who else had she been with?

As they made their way toward the water, hoping Chip hadn't concocted some reason to drive off with the airboat, Peyton's gaze drifted over the tangled vegetation surrounding them. It was then that something caught her eye—a small carving, almost hidden within the bark of a gnarled tree. She squinted and approached the tree for a closer look.

"Hey, Sean. Check this out," she called out, tracing her fingers over the intricate design.

As Sean joined her, Peyton studied the symbol. The worn carving depicted a circle, intersected by four lines arranged in an X pattern, with various smaller markings adorning the spaces between. She furrowed her brow, trying to recall if she had ever seen such a design before.

Sean leaned in closer, his brow furrowed in interest. "This is an old tribal symbol," he said, squinting at the carving. "I've seen something similar in my research, but I can't quite place it."

Peyton pulled back, examining the tree again. It was old and worn, just like the carving etched into its bark. The markings were not fresh—they had been there for a long time. And yet, they seemed subtly out of place in their surroundings. As if someone had left a coded message waiting to be discovered.

"Could it be a marker of some sort?" she asked.

"Most likely," Sean replied, his gaze still fixed on the symbol. "Tribal markings like these usually indicate boundaries or special places."

Yes, Peyton thought. *There's something special about this island, alright. It's a place of sacrifice—animal and otherwise.*

"There aren't any active tribes in this area, though," Peyton said. "I learned that during *my* research."

"Doesn't mean there isn't anyone still clinging to the old ways."

"True," Peyton conceded.

Sean pulled out his phone and took a picture of the symbol. "I'll look this up when we get back, see if I can find any information on it."

Peyton watched him for a moment, appreciating his thoroughness. Sean was meticulous in his work—it was one of the reasons they worked well together. Despite their differences – her logical, analytical approach complementing his intuition and adaptability – they had an understanding. A connection.

"Let's get moving then," Sean said, pocketing his phone.

Peyton nodded, pushing her thoughts aside. She followed Sean through the dense vegetation, their progress slow but steady. The heat was oppressive. The humidity made breathing difficult, and her muscles protested with each step she took.

Just then, as they neared the water's edge, Peyton noticed something wedged amidst the tangled mass of a cypress tree's roots. "Sean, look at this."

Sean joined her side, his eyes scanning the roots as he spotted the object of her attention—a plastic card. Carefully, Peyton extracted it, brushing away the grime to reveal the face. It was a library card, its edges frayed with use; no name adorned the card, but an ID number was clearly visible.

"Strange," Peyton muttered, holding the card up for Sean to see. "No name or anything else. Just an ID number."

Sean squinted at the card, his brow furrowing. "This is an old-school library card," he noted. "They don't make 'em like this anymore. Could be years, even decades old."

"Well, that's another mystery added to our growing list," Peyton said, tucking the card back into the weathered wallet. "I wonder where it came from?"

"Maybe we should talk to someone who knows the area, ask what libraries are around. We might get lucky."

"You two coming?" Chip suddenly called. A moment later, he emerged through the brush, swatting mosquitoes as he went.

Peyton and Sean exchanged a glance.

"Bingo," Sean said.

CHAPTER FIFTEEN

Chip turned the card over in his hands, then paused to take a swallow of sweet iced tea from his sweating glass.

"It came from a local library, no mistake," he said as he set the glass down. "That much I can say for sure."

The three of them were sitting in the only bar in town, a rustic establishment with dark wooden tables and chairs that groaned with every movement. The air was rich with the scent of beer and fried food, underscored by the muskiness of damp wood and mothball-infused cloth material. Above them, a weak fan spun lazily, moving the heavy air around but offering little relief from the Louisiana heat.

Peyton eyed Chip skeptically from across the peeling varnish of their table. Thus far, she had no reason to believe he had lied to them about anything, but the confidence with which he'd just made his assertion gave her pause.

"How can you be so sure?" she asked.

Chip shrugged nonchalantly and took another sip of his tea, his eyes never leaving the old library card. "My mother was a librarian here for thirty years," he said, his southern accent adding a languid drawl to his words. "I spent my childhood running between stacks of books, reading everything I could get my hands on."

Peyton tried to picture the grizzled swamp man in front of her, sitting in a window nook with a book spread out on his knees. She couldn't do it.

Chip carefully held up the card, inspecting it in the dim light filtering through the grimy window. "Not many people checked out books by the time she retired. Most had transitioned to digital readers or online resources." He flipped the card over again. "This was issued during her tenure. I remember seeing these cards."

Sean leaned back in his chair and ran a hand through his hair. "So, what does that tell us?"

Chip placed the card back on the table and leaned back. "I don't—you're the investigators here, ain't you?"

"It tells us,' Peyton said, "that whoever lost this card was probably local. The question is, which library did this card come from?"

"Well, that's a tricky one," Chip said. "There are several libraries in the county that it could've come from."

"Several?" Sean asked, his brows furrowed in thought. "How many are we talking about exactly?"

Chip scratched at the stubble on his chin. "I reckon about five or six that use this type of card."

Peyton felt a headache brewing at her temples. Six libraries meant hundreds, if not thousands, of potential cardholders. The task felt suddenly insurmountable.

They had to narrow down the search, ideally by eliminating five of the libraries. If they could figure out which library had issued the card, they could return to that library and discover what information the library had on file about the card's owner.

But how were they to figure out which libraries *hadn't* issued the card?

"We could go to these libraries one by one," Sean said, not sounding particularly excited.

Peyton shook her head. "It'll be too time-intensive. There has to be a better way."

She traced the rim of her glass with her finger, the ice cubes clinking against each other as she grew lost in thought. Sean sighed heavily, pulling out his cellphone and staring at the screen as if it held all the answers.

Then, suddenly, Peyton had an idea.

"Wait a minute," she said, snapping her fingers for emphasis. "You said your mother worked in one of the local libraries, right? Do you think she might remember the numbers for these ID cards? Perhaps there's a certain pattern to the numbers, a certain signature—cards from certain libraries always starting with the same numbers, for instance."

Chip chuckled, a rough sound that rippled through the semi-empty bar. "My mama? She's got a mind sharper than a gator's tooth." He took another sip from his glass. "Which is partly why I don't speak to her when I can help it."

Sean raised an eyebrow, looking intrigued and slightly amused. "Sounds like a tough woman," he said.

"You have no idea."

"If you don't want to speak with her," Peyton said, leaning forward, "then I'll do the talking. I just need her number."

Chip seemed to consider, then shook his head. "No," he said, "if anyone's gonna talk to my mama, it's gonna be. She's a spitfire, that one, and if you're not careful, she'll tear you apart without you even realizing it."

Sean let out a snort as he leaned back in his chair, crossing his arms over his chest. "And people say I'm dramatic."

"Doubt me all you want," Chip said, rubbing his weathered hands together. "You'll see soon enough." With that, he leaned to the side and dug out a grimy, ancient-looking phone—a 'dumb phone' as people called them.

He dialed a number with fingers, surprisingly nimble for their size. The air seemed to thicken as they waited. Peyton held her breath, and Sean drummed his fingers impatiently on the table, the normal hum of the bar around them sinking into a quiet murmur.

Finally, Chip cleared his throat. "Mama," he said, his voice full of respect and a hint of fear, "I need some help." He paused, wincing. "Yes, I understand it's been a long time. But, Mama—" Another pause, another wince. "No, there's nothing more important to me than family. I just haven't stopped by because...well, we always end up arguing and I...I hate fighting with you." There was a soft mutter on the other end, which made Chip's face darken. "Yeah, I remember. Not the happiest moments of my life, but I remember."

Peyton tried not to listen too closely, knowing this was not a conversation meant for her ears. However, Sean seemed to have no such qualms. His eyes were narrowed in interest, the corner of his mouth twitching with suppressed amusement.

After a few moments, Chip finally managed to steer the conversation back to their original purpose. "Mama," he said, his voice now a bit firmer than before, "I called to ask you about library cards. Remember when you used to work at the county library? You always drilled into me about how the ID numbers on cards were unique, that there was a pattern..."

There was a pause as Chip listened to the voice on the other end of the call. His expression gradually shifted from tense anticipation to relief.

"Wait, you're serious?" he asked, his eyes growing wider. "Okay, okay," he added hastily as if trying not to pause too long for fear she'd hang up on him. "So let me get this straight: The first three numbers of the card are the library prefix? Those numbers can tell us which library the card came from?"

He fell silent, listening. Peyton did her best to control her body language so she didn't show her impatience.

"One-two-one," Chip said into the phone. "Do you remember which—Miller's Library, is that right? Well, that really does help, Mama. You're a lifesaver." He paused and swallowed, nodding as if she could see him. "Yeah, I will, I promise. I'll pop by tomorrow." Another pause. "I love you, too."

Hanging up, he blew out a breath and rubbed his forehead with the back of his hand.

"Well," Sean said, trying to suppress a grin. "That sounded like fun."

"Shut it," Chip retorted, but there was no heat in it. Instead, he looked at Peyton. "That should make life a bit simpler for you."

Peyton nodded. "Miller's Library, you said?"

"That's right. It's a little ways out of town, but not hard to find."

"Thanks, Chip," Peyton said, her voice soft with gratitude. "That gives us a place to start."

He pressed his lips together, looking hesitant.

"What is it?" Peyton asked.

"It might be tricky getting access to the library records," he warned, his brow furrowing in thought. "The new manager, Kevin, is a stickler for rules. He won't be happy about the two of you showing up and asking for information about one of his members."

Peyton smiled, a twinkle in her eye. "Then we'll just have to convince him."

CHAPTER SIXTEEN

What caught Peyton's attention about Miller's Library was the intricate ironwork that adorned its entrance, depicting various scenes from classic literature. The designs were so detailed that she could make out the tiny figure of Captain Ahab locked in his eternal struggle with Moby Dick.

"Interesting choice for a library entrance," she mused aloud, her eyes following the lines of the intricate metalwork.

"Definitely unique," Sean said, admiring the craftsmanship. "Shall we go and see if the inside is even remotely as interesting?"

Peyton nodded, and together she and Sean exited the vehicle and entered the library, their footsteps loud in the hushed silence. The interior was a testament to times gone by: tall wooden shelves laden with well-worn books stood sentinel along the walls, interrupted by reading nooks with plush, burgundy chairs. A rich scent of old paper and leather bindings permeated the air, giving it a sense of nostalgia.

Despite the inviting atmosphere, however, Peyton couldn't see anyone around. She scanned the room for any signs of life, her fingers idly brushing against the edge of the library card in her pocket.

"What did Chip say the manager's name was?" she asked. "Kevin?"

Sean nodded. "Doesn't look like he's around, though."

"Let's split up," Peyton said, careful not to disturb the quiet serenity of the place. "There has to be someone working here."

Sean nodded, and he headed left while Peyton went right. They each took different aisles, scanning the books' spines and occasionally taking a minute to admire the antiquated beauty of the library.

As she moved deeper into the stacks, Peyton noticed a slight humming sound that broke the silence of the library. The sound got louder as she moved further in, and eventually, Peyton found herself standing outside a wooden door with 'Archives' written on it.

"Hello?" Peyton called.

The door was slightly ajar, revealing a space filled with books that seemed to stretch on forever. As she stepped inside, she observed the walls lined with towering bookshelves, each one cluttered with volumes that appeared to have been untouched for years. The dust that hung heavy in the air danced in a thin shaft of sunlight filtering through a grimy window. It was a small sanctuary hidden away from the world, a treasure trove of forgotten knowledge.

"Is anyone here?" Peyton asked again. Still, there was no reply. Feeling a frisson of fear trickle down her spine, she advanced farther into the room, her eyes scanning the titles on the shelves, searching for any clue that might reveal who frequented this secluded haven.

As she turned around, a figure suddenly materialized behind her, causing Peyton to cry out in shock. The figure, a gangly teenager with unruly hair and oversized glasses that magnified his wide, frightened eyes, recoiled at her reaction. His face was a map of constellations formed by acne scars, and his clothes were a haphazard combination of mismatched patterns and colors.

"Sorry, I didn't mean to scare you," the teenager stammered, removing the headphones and nestling them around his neck, oblivious to Peyton's presence until that very moment. "I was just...lost in my music."

Peyton swallowed hard, trying to regain her composure. She could feel her heart hammering against her ribcage, the adrenaline still coursing through her veins. "It's okay," she managed to say. "I was just looking for someone who works here. Do you know if there's a librarian around?"

The teenager hesitated, glancing around the room as if expecting someone else to materialize from between the stacks. "You mean Kevin?"

"Sure. Is he here?"

"Oh, he's somewhere." The teenager chuckled nervously. "He usually loses track of time when he's in the back, going through the old records. He loves all the history stuff." He trailed off.

"And you are...?"

"Oh!" He smiled, as if suddenly realizing he ought to have introduced himself. "I'm Eli. I help Kevin around here sometimes, mostly with sorting and cleaning. Not that he really notices." He shrugged, glancing around the room at the books as if they were familiar friends.

Peyton returned his smile, relieved at the apparent harmlessness of the boy. "Nice to meet you, Eli. I'm Peyton. Do you think you could fetch Kevin for me? It's somewhat urgent."

Eli blinked his wide eyes at her, pushing his glasses back up his nose with a trembling finger. "Urgent?" he repeated, the corners of his mouth dropping into a worried frown. "I, uh...he doesn't really like being interrupted, but if it's urgent..."

"Thanks, Eli." Peyton gave him an encouraging nod. He seemed to need it. With that, the spindly teenager turned and disappeared through a door at the back of the library, leaving Peyton alone in the quiet room. She took a moment to look around, taking in the tall rows of books that climbed high, almost touching the ceiling.

Every book seemed to have its place, a testament to the old librarian's love for order and history. Yet for all its order, there was a mysterious charm to the library, an air of hushed secrets nestled between the covers of each weathered tome. Peyton admired the stained-glass windows that bathed the room in dappled hues, casting colorful shadows on the polished wooden floor, and she breathed in the comforting scent of old pages.

Eli cleared his throat as he reentered the room. "Excuse me, Peyton?"

"Yes?"

"He says you can come see him. In the back." The teenager's face reddened.

Peyton was surprised by this – most librarians were happy to go out of their way to help visitors, rather than forcing visitors to come to them – but she didn't wish to make a big deal of it.

"Thank you, Eli," Peyton said with a small smile.

The teenager nodded, his wide eyes never leaving Peyton's face. He gestured toward the door from which he had just emerged and led the way, clumsily stepping over stacks of books and magazines.

They navigated through narrow aisles that snaked around the room, taking care not to disturb the looming towers of books that seemed to tremble at their slightest touch. Eli's jitteriness seemed to make him more susceptible to tripping over the uneven floorboards; every few steps, he would stumble and quickly regain his balance by reaching out for a nearby shelf. Peyton followed him with wary determination, her senses heightened by the silence enveloping the labyrinthine library.

Finally, they reached a door nestled deep within the heart of the building. Eli knocked softly, pushing open the door with a trembling hand. "Peyton," he announced in a hushed whisper, stepping aside to let her enter. Then he retreated, disappearing back the way they'd come.

The room was dim, filled with the scent of dust and aged paper that Peyton had grown accustomed to. Bookshelves lined the walls, while in the middle of the room stood a large oak table buried under layers of parchment and thick volumes. There was a charm to this chaos—an unmatched energy radiated from each artifact that Kevin had meticulously collected over the years.

There, amidst the sea of ancient texts and yellowed maps, sat a man who could only be Kevin. He was a lean figure with hunched shoulders, his eyes hidden behind a pair of round-rimmed spectacles perched precariously on the tip of his nose. Wisps of gray hair peeked out from under a threadbare cap that had seen better days.

Peyton cleared her throat, breaking the silence in the room. Kevin looked up from the time he was engrossed in, adjusting his glasses to get a clear view of Peyton.

"Eli tells me there's something urgent you need to speak with me about," he said finally. His voice was gravelly and low, as if not often used. His thin lips barely moved when he spoke.

"That's right," Peyton said as she met the man's gaze, which was as piercing as it was curious. She felt like an intruder in this sanctuary he had created. "I'm here because I need your help with something."

Kevin studied her for a moment before marking his place in the old book with a faded bookmark. He closed it with a sigh, rubbing his temples before giving Peyton his full attention. There was a coolness to his gaze as he studied her.

"I'm with the NPS," Peyton said, "and I'm working a homicide investigation. I came across this library card, and I think it may have come from this library. I need to know whose it is." She held up the library card for him to see.

"Homicide?" He let out a low whistle. "Well, I can't say people come to me very often to talk about that." He sighed, and his gaze shifted from Peyton to the card, his spectacles capturing the meager light in the room and refracting it into a shimmering dance on the aged paper.

"I don't know how this card ended up on your crime scene, but I can certainly help you find out whose it is. That is," he gave her a pointed look over his glasses, "if it is indeed from this library."

Peyton nodded, extending the card toward him. For several heartbeats, Kevin simply stared at the card in Peyton's outstretched hand before taking.

"Yes, it's from this library," he murmured as he studied the card.

"Can you scan it?" Peyton asked. "Check the database?"

"Yes," he said slowly. "I could." He paused, then looked up at her. "But that would involve sharing privileged information. It's important to me to maintain the privacy of this library's members."

"Even if they might be wrapped up in a homicide investigation?" Peyton asked, surprised by his resistance.

He shrugged. "It doesn't change one's right to privacy, does it?"

"The person who owned that card could be dead," Peyton said, growing frustrated. "Or the person who owns it could be the murderer."

Just then, Peyton heard the sound of approaching footsteps and turned around to see Sean.

"Ah, you have him," Sean said. "Have you been able to figure out whose library card it is?"

"No," Peyton said, pressing her lips together firmly. "Kevin here doesn't want to intrude on anyone's privacy."

"Ah," Sean said, nodding. "Well, that's very noble of you, Kevin. Very noble. But, you see, if you make us go find a judge and get a warrant—well, it'll cost time, but it also might cost someone their life."

Kevin frowned. "What do you mean?"

"I mean that someone else's life might be in danger," Sean said. "I promise we have grounds for getting that warrant, but if we can avoid that, it will save precious time. We need your help, Kevin."

Kevin stared at the two NPS officers, and for a long moment, silence reigned in the room. His gaze then drifted back to the card in his hands. He flipped it over a few times before heaving a deep sigh.

His fingers played with the edge of the card as he turned to Peyton. "I never thought I'd see the day when a library card would be linked to something so grim," he said in an almost whispered voice.

"In our line of work," Peyton answered, "everything is a potential link."

"Alright," Kevin relented, his thin lips flattening. "I'll do it. Only because it might help save a life." He stood slowly, the creak of old bones matching the groan of the worn floorboards beneath him. "Follow me."

He led them through a labyrinth of towering bookshelves, each crammed with books that ranged from ancient and leather-bound to glossy and modern. The scent of yellowed paper and ink seemed stronger in the heart of the library, as if all knowledge collected there had become a vapor that hung in the air.

Finally, they reached an alcove where a dust-covered computer sat. Kevin took his seat and began to work, his fingers dancing over the keyboard with surprising speed. The computer sprang to life, its screen casting a cold, blue glow over Kevin's face as he logged into the library database.

"Let's see," he murmured, entering the digits from the library card into the search bar. Peyton and Sean exchanged glances as they waited with bated breath, the steady hum of the computer filling the air.

Suddenly, Kevin stopped and peered at the screen, his spectacles reflecting the pale light harshly. "Here we are," he said slowly as he read aloud from the screen. "The card belongs to a..." He leaned forward to read it. "Levi M. Alon. Huh. Strange name."

Sean frowned, tilting his head slightly as he studied the screen. Then suddenly he laughed.

"What?" Peyton asked, surprised.

"Leave me alone. The name means, 'leave me alone.' It's fake."

Peyton shook her head, unsure what to make of this. She turned back to Kevin. "Is there an address listed for this 'Levi Alon'?"

"Yes, there is," Kevin said, scrolling down the screen until the relevant information came into view. "It's right here: 3825 Bayou Road."

"Thank you for your help," Peyton said, offering the librarian a grateful smile. "We appreciate it."

"Of course—that's what librarians are for. Helping." He paused, frowning.

"What is it?" Peyton asked.

"You'll want to be careful. Bayou Road isn't exactly the best part of town."

"How so?" Sean asked.

"Well, it's...y'know, the kind of place where things go missing and people don't ask too many questions," the librarian replied, pushing his glasses up the bridge of his nose. "It's old and rundown—not a pleasant place to visit."

Peyton could feel a knot of unease form in her stomach as she exchanged glances with Sean.

"Thanks for the warning," Sean said. "We'll keep our wits about us."

As they left the musty library behind, stepping back into the bright light of day, Peyton felt a stirring of unease. She looked down at the fading library card in her hand again. Levi M. Alon—a fake name and an ominous address.

Could this be the killer's card?

CHAPTER SEVENTEEN

Afternoon was creeping toward evening as Peyton and Sean pulled up to the address listed on the library card. The house before them was a decrepit structure, its wooden walls rotting away under the weight of years of neglect. Vines crawled up the sides, weaving through the cracked windows like fingers clutching desperately at the crumbling framework. Moss hung from the sagging roof, giving the impression that the entire building was being slowly consumed by the surrounding wilderness.

"Doesn't look like anyone's been here for a while," Peyton said, her eyes scanning the dilapidated building with a mixture of curiosity and unease. "You sure this is the right place?"

"According to the information we got from Kevin," Sean replied, his blue eyes narrowed as he studied the house. "But if you ask me, it's more likely a dead end than anything else."

"Only one way to find out," Peyton said, stepping out of the car with a determined stride. Sean followed without argument, shutting the car door quietly behind him.

She made her way toward the wooden steps that led to the front door. Each step felt heavy, as if the grim aura of the house itself was trying to pull her back. The wind whistled, carrying an eerie melody that reminded Peyton of a long-lost lullaby. She shook off the feeling and continued forward.

A short distance away, hidden by a screen of mangroves, she could hear the sounds of the swamp: the chorus of croaking frogs, the gentle gurgle of water, and the rustle of unseen creatures in the underbrush. The house seemed to be an abandoned outpost at the edge of the wild, forgotten by time and people.

"Hello?" she called out hesitantly, raising a hand to knock on the warped front door. There was no response, just the faint creaking of the aging wood and the distant chirping of cicadas in the trees. She knocked again, louder this time, but still received no answer.

"Maybe 'Levi' isn't home," Sean said dryly. "Wouldn't be surprised to learn he's abandoned the place altogether."

"Either way, I think we need to take a look inside," Peyton insisted, her gaze fixed on the house. "We need to know who the card belongs to."

"And how do you suggest we get in?"

Peyton thought about it. "You stay here in case anyone comes to the door. I'll head around back, see if there's another entrance."

Sean shrugged and knocked on the door again.

Peyton began circling the house. It didn't take long before she noticed a back door leaning precariously in its frame, the hinges rusted and broken.

"This should do it," she said. She considered going back and telling Sean what she'd found, but it was probably better for him to stay out front. If she confronted someone in the house, and that someone tried to run, it would be good for Sean to have one of the exits covered.

The door creaked open. The moment Peyton crossed the threshold, a heavy mustiness assaulted her nostrils. She wrinkled her nose in disgust as she took in the dim interior of the rundown house. The paint on the walls was peeling and stained with brownish streaks from water damage, and the floorboards creaked ominously beneath her weight. Cobwebs hung from the corners, their silken threads swaying gently in the stale air.

Who would live in a place like this? Peyton thought as she cautiously moved deeper into the house.

She made her way past stacks of yellowing newspapers and piles of tattered books, realizing that the disarray extended beyond simple neglect. Her eyes were drawn to a makeshift altar set up against one wall. The table was adorned with black candles and an assortment of bizarre trinkets, including a skull and an ancient-looking dagger. But what truly gave Peyton pause were the strange symbols etched into the wood and smeared onto the wall behind it—undeniably occultic signs.

And there, she thought, her breath catching in her throat. *That's the symbol we saw on the island.*

She drew her gun, moving cautiously through the house until she found herself standing before a locked door, its surface marred by deep scratches and gouges. Curiosity gnawed at her, urging her to find a way in.

She reached a hand out to the handle, but found it cold and unyielding. Frozen, she listened. The only sounds were the distant chirp of the cicadas and her own shallow breathing.

Coming to a sudden decision, she gave the door a hard kick. The rusted lock snapped and the door flew open. The room inside was devoid of any furniture, save for a single desk sitting in the center. Atop it sat a dusty desktop computer, its monitor blank and uninviting.

"Sean!" she called, directing her voice toward the front of the house. "I think I found something!"

She waited, but no answer came. "Sean?" As she turned to head to the front door and let Sean in, she accidentally bumped the desk, causing the monitor to come to life.

She stared at the login screen. The screen stared back, the little box waiting for her to fill in the password.

If this was the killer's computer...what secrets might it hold?

Coming to a decision, she decided to search the room and see if she could find a clue to the password anywhere.

Everything in the room seemed to have been deliberately stripped back, as though the person using it were uninterested in personal comforts. The walls were bare of any sort of decoration, and the floor was nothing but cracked and dusty tiles. It gave her the sense of a location used purely for necessity rather than any personal comfort or enjoyment.

Which also meant there weren't many places a password could be hidden.

She decided to look through the drawers of the desk first, pulling them open one by one. They didn't contain much – a collection of pens, a pile of paperclips, some notepads filled with indecipherable scribbles – but then she pulled out a small leather-bound notebook from the bottom drawer. Peyton opened it up, flicking through pages filled with notes written in a rushed and almost unreadable scrawl.

Then, her fingers paused on a page. She squinted at it, eyes narrowing as she focused on what was written. There were a number of passwords, and she started trying them one by one. After a number of failed attempts, she entered 'GatorBaiter79' and was relieved to see the desktop screen appear.

"Gotcha," she muttered under her breath.

The desktop was surprisingly tidy, with only a handful of folders and icons scattered across the dark screen. There were a few video games and movies, but otherwise it appeared the computer got very little use. Peyton clicked on the email icon at the bottom.

Is this computer even online? she wondered. She checked the bottom right corner of her screen. No, apparently not. These emails must be old.

Peyton came across a number of emails written to someone named

Leah. The last email read,

Leah,

I thought you should know, and I don't know how to say this any way but straight up: the old man passed away. Got bit by a gator while he was out fishing. It's like something straight out of a horror movie, I swear, only it's real life and it's my life.

He refused to get the bite looked at. You know how he was, stubborn as a mule and twice as ornery. It turned septic. Next thing we knew, he was gone. Just like that.

I wish you could've met him. I think you two would've gotten along. Thanks for listening,

Patrick

"Patrick," Peyton mused. Could the email have been written by Patrick Sharma, one of the victims? It would make sense. If that was the case, then that meant this was probably his house, and the library card was probably his, too—the one Peyton and Sean had found on the 'haunted' island Jennifer Easton had also visited.

Peyton went on reading the emails. The strangest part of it all was that Patrick hadn't sent these emails, but rather saved them to his Drafts folder. Peyton got the impression that Leah was an estranged sister, or perhaps half-sister, of Patrick's.

Peyton felt a strange sense of unease as she read through the emails. There was an air of sadness and regret that made her feel like she was prying into someone's personal life, which she technically was. Part of her job required this sort of invasion, but it didn't make it any easier.

The important thing is that I now know the library card belonged to Patrick Sharma, she thought. *He was on that island, just like Jennifer was. Maybe the island is the common thread among all the victims.*

She needed to head back outside and share her findings with Sean. She was a bit surprised he hadn't come looking for her and seen the back door, but maybe he was still keeping an eye out in case the owner of the house – Patrick Sharma, as Peyton now knew – returned.

Walking back through the abandoned house, Peyton realized that she felt different from when she'd entered. It was a peculiar sensation, as though she'd trespassed upon a forbidden history and emerged with stolen knowledge. Yet, her resolve remained unbroken.

She took one last look at the bare room and noticed something she hadn't before: a small photo frame turned upside down on the desk.

Picking it up, she discovered a faded photo of a smiling man in his late 20s. He stood next to an older man who bore an uncanny resemblance to him, both holding fishing rods. The corners of Peyton's mouth twitched into a small smile as she realized it must have been Patrick and his father, the stubborn old man who'd been taken by a gator, according to the unsent emails. As sad as it was, there was a hint of warmth, of shared memories preserved in this single image.

She gently placed the photo back onto the desk, making sure it was right side up this time. She cast a fleeting glance toward the still-glowing monitor, a silent eulogy to a life she'd never known but had reached into.

Exiting the room, she found her way out of the house as silent as a ghost. The sun was hanging low in the sky now, casting long shadows that made the dilapidated house look even more eerie and desolate. The cicadas were quieter than they had been before, but the frogs were just as loud, filling the Louisiana swamps with their song.

Still thinking about Patrick's emails, Peyton made her way around to the front of the house. She was surprised, however, to find Sean missing.

"Sean?" she called, puzzled. Where had he gone? The Jeep was still here, so he couldn't have left. Peyton felt her heart rate increase slightly, a thin layer of cold sweat forming at the base of her neck. The descending sun was no longer warm on her skin, but rather cold and indifferent.

She walked up the steps to the porch. "Sean?" she called again, louder this time. Her voice slipped through the open windows of the run-down home, unanswered. An unsettling tickle crept up the back of her spine; something wasn't right.

Peyton quickly moved to the Jeep, hoping he might be inside escaping the stinging insects. But a quick glance through the window confirmed it was empty. She felt a twinge of panic. Had something happened while she had been immersed in Patrick's emails?

"Damn it, Sean, where are you?" she muttered under her breath as she circled the house, hoping to find a trace of him. She was about to call out his name again when she heard a faint noise overpowering the chorus of the frogs. What was that, an engine of some kind? Maybe an airboat?

She turned her attention toward the screen of mangroves that grew thickly behind the house, blocking her view of the water. Carefully, she approached the edge of the swamp, the sounds now louder, a persistent low drone. She fought her way through the undergrowth, ignoring the insects crawling across her skin, trying not to think about the cottonmouth she'd nearly been bitten by earlier.

As she neared the water, the drone of the engine began to recede. She pushed through a screen of grass just in time to see an airboat disappearing behind a strip of mangroves draped with Spanish moss, the algae-covered water undulating in its wake.

What the hell is going on? Where's Sean?

Peyton felt her chest tighten as she watched the airboat grow smaller and smaller before it disappeared completely out of sight. It was then she saw it: a hint of blue fabric tangled in one of the mangroves. She moved closer and pulled it loose.

It was a piece of Sean's shirt.

CHAPTER EIGHTEEN

Peyton stood by the window of the precinct, her eyes scanning the dark outstretch of the moonlit swamp.

Where are you, Sean? she thought.

She had spent over an hour searching for Sean around Patrick Sharma's house but found no sign of him. Now she was in Officer Dayton Wilder's office, hoping he might be able to help her find her missing partner.

Wilder leaned against his desk, studying her thoughtfully, as if unsure what to say. His burly frame and blue eyes had seemed reassuring before, but now they appeared distant and unhelpful.

"We have to find him," Peyton said in a hollow voice. "I can't just stand here while he's out there somewhere."

"I understand your concern," replied Wilder, his scarred cheek twitching. "But it's late, and we've already searched the area thoroughly. We're doing everything we can."

"Doing everything?" Peyton asked, her frustration building. "We should be out there right now, searching the swamps and trying to figure out where that airboat went—not sitting in here, hoping he turns up." She felt guilty for having left Patrick's house, despite having spent an hour there in a fruitless search. She didn't know whether the airboat had anything to do with Sean's disappearance...but then again, it seemed like a strange coincidence.

"Listen, Peyton, the swamps are dangerous at night," Wilder said. "There are poachers, alligators, even drug runners. We can't risk it."

"But we can risk Sean's life?" Peyton shot back, her hands clenching and unclenching nervously as her mind raced with terrifying possibilities.

Wilder sighed heavily, running a hand through his graying hair. "I didn't say that. But you have to understand our limitations here."

"Mighty convenient limitations."

"Listen," Wilder said, his tone softening a bit, "I know you're worried about him. We all are. But we'll start the search as soon as daylight breaks."

Peyton stared at him, her eyes blazing with fear and frustration. His words did nothing to assuage her growing fear. Tension coiled within her like a spring ready to release.

"He's out there, in the dark, possibly hurt," she said softly, her voice choked with emotion. "And I'm supposed to just wait?"

She turned back to the window, the murky landscape of the swamp seeming even more ominous under the moonlit glow. Somewhere out there, Sean was lost...or worse.

Wilder sighed once more and leaned back in his chair. "Are you sure he didn't go to check on another lead?"

"We only had one vehicle. Besides, he's not answering his phone. And that piece of his shirt..." She swallowed hard, preferring not to imagine what might have happened.

The silence lengthened.

"He *is* a wilderness survival expert," Wilder said. Peyton had the impression he was trying to think of some way to comfort her, some way to imply this situation wasn't as bad as she thought.

"He is," Peyton agreed. "But he's not used to swamps. He's spent his career in mountains, deserts, forests...not wetlands. He's from Montana, for goodness' sake. He doesn't know this terrain."

Wilder steepled his fingers and pursed his lips, the very picture of a man choosing his words delicately. "We'll only put more people in danger if we send out a search party now," he said. "But as I said before, when the sun comes up—"

"I can't wait that long," Peyton said, turning away from the window as she came to a decision. "I'm going back out there. I have to figure out where the airboat went."

"Going out there alone is too dangerous," Wilder replied, his brow furrowed with concern. "There are a lot of poachers in the area, and they won't hesitate to shoot first and ask questions later."

"Then can Chip take me?" Peyton asked hopefully, thinking of the experienced local guide who had shown them around earlier.

"Chip's already gone home for the night," Wilder explained. "Besides, he's a hard man to reach—doesn't like having his phone on."

Chip, Peyton thought, recalling her earlier suspicions about the guide. Was he out there somewhere with Sean right now? Had he attacked Sean?

"How well do you know your brother-in-law?" she asked Wilder.

He cocked his head curiously at her. "Why do you ask?"

Peyton decided not to pull any punches. "He's a guide, right? Knows these swamps well."

"Yes..." Wilder drew the word out, waiting for a further explanation.

"Jennifer Easton was looking for a guide, someone to show her the swamps—she owned a marketing consultancy firm, wanted to see what opportunities there were for tourism here. And I think that whoever took her out into the swamps was the person who killed her." She paused, letting her words sink in.

"I still don't get what this has to do with Chip," Wilder said.

"There's an island out there, an island surrounded by a lot of superstition. Well, two of the victims ended up on that island, and I have a suspicion the other two might have been there as well. And who better to know their way around such a place than a local guide with extensive knowledge of the swamps?"

"Like Chip, you mean." Wilder's voice was as flat as his desk.

"I'm not saying I know anything for certain," Peyton said, "but we need to explore every possibility. That's why I asked how well you know him."

"You think my brother-in-law is a serial killer."

"I think we need to consider every possibility." Peyton could tell by the tone in Wilder's voice that she was losing him. *Why is he taking this so personally?* she thought. *Doesn't he realize he needs to put his own feelings aside for the good of the investigation?*

Wilder's eyes became slits, and his jaw tightened. "My brother-in-law isn't some murderous psychopath."

Peyton held up her hands in a calming gesture, attempting to pacify the suddenly defensive officer. "I get it. Family is important, and it's hard to imagine someone you care about could do such things, but we can't ignore the facts."

His icy gaze bored into hers. The silence stretched between them, taut and heavy.

"Look," Peyton began after what felt like an eternity, "if you're convinced he's innocent, then prove it to me. Prove that he couldn't have committed the murders, that he doesn't fit the profile—just give me something."

"I don't have to give you anything," Wilder retorted, rising from his chair. The softening effect of his earlier sympathies had evaporated. His face was composed of rigid lines and harsh angles. "This is my town, my investigation. I'll decide who is a suspect and who isn't."

Peyton felt the sting of his words, but she wouldn't be bullied into submission. She straightened her back, her stance defiant. "Your town, your investigation," she echoed, unable to keep the bitterness from seeping into her voice. "And yet, you haven't made any progress. Four people are dead, and now my partner is missing."

"You don't think I'm doing my job?" His voice was low, dangerous, but Peyton wasn't intimidated.

"I think you're too close to this," she said. "You're biased, allowing personal relationships to cloud your judgment."

"And you're not biased? Your partner goes missing, and suddenly you're pointing the finger at my family?" Wilder's words were sharp, cutting through the tense silence of the room.

Peyton stepped closer to Wilder, the gap between them seeming both literal and metaphorical at once. "No one wants to find Sean more than I do," Peyton said firmly. "But I'm not going to let personal feelings stop me from considering every potential lead."

Wilder stared at her for a long moment before shaking his head in disbelief. "I don't know what kind of operation you're used to running," he said, his voice heavy with scorn, "but we do things differently here."

"I'm aware of how you do things here, Wilder." Peyton's words were laced with impatience. "And that's exactly why I'm here."

The two of them stood there, locked in a silent standoff. The ticking of the clock on the wall seemed louder in the quiet office, each second reminding Peyton that Sean could be in terrible danger that very moment, and instead of looking for him, she was here at the precinct arguing with Wilder.

This was foolish.

She sighed, rubbing a weary hand over her forehead. "I'm sorry if that came across as an attack," she said. "I'm not trying to frame Chip. It's just...if you could help me clear him of suspicion, if you could help me see why there's no reason at all to suspect him..."

Wilder stared off into space for a few seconds. Then his face softened.

"Alright," he conceded, pinching the bridge of his nose. "I understand where you're coming from. Chip has been a pain in my ass since we were kids, but he's not a killer." He leaned back against his desk, crossing his arms over his chest.

Looking into his eyes, Peyton could see the strain of the situation etched in them. As much as he wanted to defend his family, he also understood the pressing nature of the investigation. He had lives to protect too.

"Chip wasn't even in the state for the first two murders earlier this month," he said. "He was up north, on a hunting trip with some buddies. And for the third one...he was here, with us at the station, dealing with an issue about his fishing license."

"And the fourth?"

"He and I were having dinner with our families. I can vouch for him."

Peyton nodded, feeling a weight lift off her shoulders. "Alright," she said. "That's more like it." She looked at him and added, "I have always believed in innocent until proven guilty."

"Good to hear," Wilder said. His tone was gruff, but Peyton thought she saw relief in his eyes.

It occurred to Peyton then that Wilder might just be protecting his brother. Was it possible they were both involved in the murders? Had Chip done something terrible, and now Wilder was covering for him?

No, she thought. *Now you're getting paranoid. If you go down that rabbit hole, you'll just waste more precious time—time Sean might not have.*

She would simply have to trust Wilder. She didn't know him very well, but she considered herself a fairly good judge of character, and Wilder struck her as a man with few secrets.

She sighed and nodded, coming to a decision. "Well, if Chip can't take me out into the swamps, then I'll need to borrow an airboat."

Wilder's eyebrows pulled together in a quizzical frown. "Have you ever driven an airboat before?"

"No," Peyton said, feeling a wave of determination washing over her. "But how hard can it be?"

"That's not the point," Wilder replied, shaking his head. "It's not just about driving an airboat. It's about navigating the swamps safely, avoiding the dangers."

"Dangers that Sean is facing right now." Peyton's gaze was steady on Wilder, her fear replaced by a steely resolve.

"Peyton." Wilder sighed. "I admire your courage, but this is foolhardy. I am responsible for your safety as long as you're here."

"And I'm responsible for Sean. We're partners—we have each other's backs."

"I can't give you an airboat," Wilder insisted, his voice firm. But his eyes held a look of regret. "It's against the department's regulations."

"Then I'll find another way," Peyton said. "But I'm not waiting until morning."

Wilder studied her for a moment. Earlier, when they'd first met, he'd struck her as an agreeable man, eager to please. Now, however, she saw the steel in his gaze, the rigid set of his jaw. He was not going to be swayed.

"You're going to get yourself killed," Wilder said, his tone dark.

"Maybe," Peyton admitted, her eyes not leaving his. "But if I do nothing, Sean might die."

For a moment, Wilder looked like he was going to argue. But then he sighed, sinking back into his chair.

"Alright," he said eventually. "I can't stop you from going out there. But I won't be a part of it. And I won't provide you with an airboat."

"I understand," Peyton replied, nodding stiffly. She felt a grim satisfaction—at least she'd managed to make him see reason.

"But I'm warning you, Peyton," Wilder added, pointing a stern finger at her. "If anything happens to you out there...it's on your own head."

Peyton swallowed hard but nodded again. "I'll take that risk." She turned toward the door, then paused. "Oh, and you should know something, too."

He waited.

"If anything happens to Sean because you were too slow to send out a search party," she said, "that's on *your* head."

CHAPTER NINETEEN

Peyton slammed the door shut behind her as she left the office—a bit childish, perhaps, but it felt good nonetheless. She was halfway to the door leading outside, still without a plan, when she noticed the rack of keys on the wall.

Airboat keys.

Peyton glanced back toward Wilder's office. She could hear him shuffling papers around, oblivious to her actions. She felt a twinge of guilt at what she was about to do, but it was quickly quashed by a surge of urgency. It was Sean's life at stake here.

Without wasting another moment, she made her way over to the rack of keys, scanning them quickly. Each key was labeled with small, neat letters etched into metal tags. Most were for various structures in the compound, but there were a few marked with the names of the airboats.

"The Gator Queen," Peyton muttered under her breath, recognizing the name from their initial tour of the facility. Purposefully, she snatched the key off its hook and pocketed it.

She had just turned to leave when she heard Wilder's voice cut through the silence behind her.

"Peyton." His tone was sharp and full of warning.

She froze, hand still on the doorknob.

He sighed deeply. "Do you know what the consequences are for stealing an airboat?" Wilder asked. His voice sounded neutral. There was no anger in it.

"Right now, I don't care," Peyton said, her hand still clutching the key in her pocket. "I'll face those consequences later."

"What you're doing is not just illegal, it's suicidal," he said. "You have no idea how fast the weather can change out there or how many gators lie waiting."

"I'll take my chances," Peyton replied stubbornly. "Every minute we waste arguing, Sean's chances get slimmer."

"Peyton," Wilder pleaded, sounding worn out. "Think about this rationally. If you get stranded out there or, God forbid, get hurt...you won't be helping Sean at all. You'll be another person we have to

95

rescue."

"Which would force you to put yourself in danger, right? What a shame that would be."

Wilder's face colored. He looked embarrassed rather than angry.

"I'm going now," Peyton said, opening the door.

"Wait!"

Peyton looked back.

"You're not going to find him alone," Wilder said, looking resigned. "At the very least, let me give you some guidance on navigating the swamps." He walked over to a slide-out map of the area that was tacked to the wall.

"This is the location of the house you were at, 3825 Bayou Road," he said, pointing to a section of waterway etched into the map. "The currents around there are unpredictable, especially with the recent storms." Peyton watched as his finger traced a path around several obstacles. "There's a section over here that's less treacherous, but it will add time to your route."

"I don't care about time," she said. "Just tell me how to get there."

He looked at her, eyes filled with worry but also something else...respect? "Follow this path until you reach this bend." He tapped on an area of the map etched in blue ink. "Then turn south-east and steer clear of these cypress trees, their roots rise above water level and can capsize your boat."

"Got it." Peyton nodded, doing her best to memorize the route he had outlined. "Anything else?"

"Watch out for the sawgrass clusters," he added. "They're sharp—they'll mess you up if you get tangled in them."

Peyton swallowed hard, taking in the array of dangers that awaited her. It was a lot to remember, but she would do whatever it took to find Sean.

"Thank you," she said, meeting his gaze. There was more she wanted to say, but time was not on her side. "I have to go."

Wilder nodded, stepping back. "Be careful, Peyton," he said, his voice thick with concern. "And...good luck."

Peyton turned and left without another word, clutching the key tightly in her hand.

True to his word, Wilder didn't try to stop her as she found her way toward the dock where 'The Gator Queen' sat bobbing gently in the murky waters. The airboat was large and sturdy, capable of tackling any obstacle the swamp might throw at her.

As she climbed into the boat, Wilder's warnings echoed in her mind. She tightened her grip on the steering stick and started the powerful engine. The boat roared to life beneath her.

Peyton took a moment to gather herself. She could almost feel Sean's presence beside her, giving her strength.

She took a deep breath and pushed the throttle forward, setting the airboat in motion. Its flat bottom skimmed over the water with ease, sending sprays of muddy liquid out to either side. The wind whipped through her hair as she navigated past the moored boats, leaving the precinct behind.

A cacophony of sounds filled the air around her: the hum of insects above the water's surface; the calls of birds hidden amid tree branches; the persistent thrumming of the airboat's engine. Peyton navigated through waterways draped with Spanish moss, their dreamlike beauty belying the dangers that lurked beneath.

The sky began to darken. Lightning streaked across the sky in jagged veins, thunder echoing ominously overhead. Rain began to pelt her, stinging against her skin as she increased her speed, pushing 'The Gator Queen' harder.

Plumes of spray arched away from the boat as she raced down wild and winding channels, her muscles straining against the constant buffeting of wind and rain. Each roar of thunder made Peyton's heart pound faster in her chest, her senses heightened by the adrenaline coursing through her veins.

To her left was a sudden hiss, and a dark shape slithered into the water. A gator. Peyton flinched, but kept her eyes fixed on the path ahead, using the dim light provided by the flashes of lightning.

She knew that she would have to stop soon. The rain was falling harder now, droplets hammering against her skin with such force that it was starting to hurt. She was soaked to the bone and shivering from the cold, but she ignored it all. Her focus was on finding Sean.

Suddenly, the boat lurched violently. Peyton was thrown forward, her knuckles whitening as she clung to the steering stick. She glanced back and saw a large cluster of sawgrass tangled around the propeller. The sawgrass Wilder had warned her about.

Cursing herself for not paying better attention, she struggled to slow down, finally managing to kill the engine. She let out a shaky breath as she unclipped her seatbelt and made her way toward the back of the boat. The sawgrass was tangled tightly around the propeller, the sharp blades glistening ominously in the sporadic lightning.

Ignoring the biting cold and tugging pain from where she'd been thrown against the steering stick, Peyton crouched down in the slimy, rain-soaked bottom of the boat. She pulled a knife from her boot, steeling herself for the task ahead. This was going to be difficult and time-consuming, but she had to do it.

Her fingers felt numb against the metal handle of the knife, but she gripped it tightly, sawing at the serrated edges of the sawgrass. The rain seemed to be falling even harder now, drumming against the boat like a relentless symphony. Despite everything, Peyton couldn't help but marvel at the harsh beauty of the swamp under the storm's siege.

She worked in silence, eyes narrowed in concentration as she slowly disentangled each blade of grass from around the propeller. By the time she finished, her hands were bloodied and blistered. Her body screamed with exhaustion, and her clothes clung wetly to her skin. It was dangerous to be out in such a storm (what would happen if she couldn't get the boat moving again?), but despite all this, she found herself feeling incredibly alive.

As she finished with the sawgrass, she straightened and prepared to start the engine again. Just then, however, she noticed something in the water beside her, a log she hadn't noticed before.

A log with a pair of yellow, hungry eyes.

CHAPTER TWENTY

The strangest part about the alligator, Peyton realized as a jolt of adrenaline flooded her system, was the patch of blood on the side of its head.

It's been shot, Peyton thought, recalling Wilder's warning about poachers in this area. Fear and disbelief knotted inside her. She reached for the gun she'd packed, only to find the holster empty. Her heart hammered as she frantically searched the boat's floor, feeling a wave of relief when her fingers closed around the cold metal.

The gator inched closer, its eyes never leaving Peyton. It made no sudden movements, as if it sensed her desperation. With numb fingers, Peyton raised the gun, aiming at the yellow-eyed predator.

"Please don't," she whispered to the storm and the beast in front of her. She didn't want to have to fire—partly because she didn't want to kill this creature, and partly because she wasn't sure if a single bullet would do the trick. Clearly, this gator had taken a licking and went on ticking.

Peyton backed away, the boat creaking beneath her. The gator merely watched her, as if undecided about what it should do. All it would take was one lunge, and it would be in the boat. Then she would have no choice but to fire.

Just then, Peyton glimpsed something—a searchlight only a few hundred yards away, drifting closer. Three figures, barely visible in the dimness of the night, scanned their surroundings, shotguns in their hands.

Searching for the wounded gator, no doubt.

Now it was imperative Peyton didn't fire. If she alerted those poachers to her presence, she would become a much easier target than the alligator. And if they learned she was with the National Park Service – law enforcement, in other words – what were her chances of making it out of this swamp alive?

Her heart pounded against her ribcage as she crouched low in the boat, keeping herself out of sight. She held the gun firmly, her finger hovering over the trigger.

Keep going, she thought, hoping the weeds around the boat would conceal it from the poachers. *Please don't see us.*

The poachers began to slow, their flashlights cutting through the night and bouncing off the rain-soaked foliage. Peyton could hear their muffled voices over the drumming rain but couldn't make out what they were saying. She dared not move or even breathe too loudly. Even the gator seemed to sense the danger, its yellow eyes flickering between Peyton and the approaching poachers.

The boat creaked softly underneath her as she shifted her weight, trying to keep herself hidden. She attempted to steady her shaky hands, eyes watching as one of the poachers moved the searchlight closer to her position.

Panic began clawing at her chest, making it hard to breathe. *Take it easy,* she told herself. *It's going to be okay.* The words, however, felt hollow. She knew all too well how dangerous this situation was.

Snatches of conversation drifted over the water toward Peyton.

"They were out here earlier, too," a phlegmy voice said. "Two of them Feds, just moseying around like they owned the place."

"What was they after?" a second, this one sounding younger than the first, asked.

"Prob'ly after you on account of what you did to that lady friend of yours."

There was a chorus of gruff laughter at this.

"Ah, shut your pie-hole," the younger one said sulkily. "She had it coming."

She? Peyton thought. *Could he be talking about Jennifer Easton? Could these poachers have had something to do with her death?*

Suddenly, a brilliant crack of lightning illuminated the swamp in silver light. For a terrifying moment, Peyton thought for certain the poachers had seen her. Then their boat glided past her, less than twenty feet away, and she breathed a sigh of relief, grateful for the protection of the tall grass.

Peyton straightened. She turned her attention back to the gator...but it was gone now. She peered around, wondering if perhaps it had just sunk beneath the water, but she couldn't see it anywhere.

Meanwhile, the poachers were slowly drifting away. Peyton realized she needed to speak with them and learn what they knew. But if she started up the airboat, they would hear her immediately—and then they would probably gun her down. She was outnumbered three-to-one, after all.

Then I'll have to get the drop on them, she thought, eyeing the dark water. *I'll just have to swim.*

But what about the gator? What if it was lurking nearby, just waiting for her?

Before she could second guess her decision, Peyton had already slipped out of her boots and was perched on the edge of the boat. She took one last deep breath, filling her lungs with the damp, earthy air of the swamp before plunging into the water.

The feel of the cool water sent a jolt of fear through her. Her instincts were screaming at her to get out, but she fought against them. Keeping low, she began to swim toward the poachers' boat making sure to keep her movements controlled to avoid creating ripples in the water. Each time something brushed against her leg, she had to fight back a shiver of fear, thinking it might be the gator coming to finish what it had started.

The voices of the poachers grew louder as she approached their boat. Peyton kept herself underwater as much as possible to avoid being seen. She emerged from the water behind their boat silently as a ghost. Her fingers gripped onto the edge of it, and slowly, inch by inch, she pulled herself up, peering over the side to take stock of her enemies.

One man was at the tiller, while two others were laughing and drinking from a shared bottle. They wore grimy clothes that had seen better days, their faces unshaven, and their eyes filled with a cruel hardness. She recognized the sullen young man from his voice—his squashed nose and thick brow gave him an oafish appearance that belied a certain cunning in his eyes. The oldest one, with a grizzled beard and rheumy eyes, was surely the one who'd made the crude joke about the woman. The third man – bald and burly – was the silent type.

None of the three were looking in her direction. All she had to do was hang on and listen, hoping they would keep talking about the woman they'd mentioned.

"Probably floating belly-up in one of these inlets," the one with the grizzled beard was saying. "We'll find him, boys. It was a good shot."

Peyton cursed silently. They were talking about the gator, not the woman they'd mentioned. She considered holding on longer, hoping the conversation would circle back, but she felt an urge to act. Her hands were aching from holding onto the boat, and she knew that with every passing second, the chance of her being discovered increased. She needed to climb up, disarm them, and then question them about Jennifer Easton. It was a risky plan, but she had no other choice.

Taking a deep breath, her gun in one hand, she pulled herself up onto the back of the boat.

The poachers didn't notice her at first. The youngest was in the middle of a hearty laugh when he finally spotted Peyton out of the corner of his eye. His laughter came to an abrupt halt, his eyes widening in shock. "What the—"

The older two men were on their feet instantly, reaching for their firearms.

"Touch them and you die!" Peyton said. "Nobody move!"

CHAPTER TWENTY ONE

She leveled her gun, her hand steady despite the circumstances. She had the element of surprise now, but it wouldn't last long. If she were going to learn anything about Jennifer Easton's death from these men, she would have to act quickly.

The youngest poacher's eyes flicked toward his shotgun propped against the side of the boat before returning to Peyton. He raised his hands slowly, a cunning glint in his eyes belying his feigned innocence. The burly man's gaze was fixed on her, studying, calculating. Only the eldest seemed genuinely terrified, his rheumy eyes wide and darting nervously between Peyton and the gun in her hand.

"Who are you?" the young man blurted out, breaking the tense silence that had descended over them.

"NPS," Peyton said. "Now I'll be asking the questions. Who was that woman you were talking about earlier? The one you said 'had it coming'?"

The younger man's eyes flickered for a moment, his confidence wavering. "I dunno what you're talking about, lady," he said, trying to keep a semblance of bravado.

"Don't play dumb," Peyton snapped. "I heard you. You were talking about a woman who had it coming."

"Ah, that," the young man said dismissively. "We was just messing, talking shit. Nothing important."

Peyton's gaze narrowed as she studied him. He was lying, that much she was sure of. But how much was he hiding?

"You're bluffing," the burly man said. "That gun was in the water—it won't fire properly."

"You want to test your theory?" Peyton wasn't sure if he was right or not, but she sure as hell wasn't going to lower the weapon.

"She was my ex, okay?" the younger man said. "Tess Ballard."

"What happened to her?"

He hesitated, clearly uncomfortable.

"I can wait all night if I have to," Peyton said, though she wasn't sure this was true. She was drenched, and the night air seemed to be cooling by the minute. If she dropped her guard for a single second, she would probably be dead within the minute.

"You know what?" she said as a new idea struck her. "Go ahead, pick up your weapons. I want you to toss them over the side."

The burly man sneered. "You're joking."

"Not one bit."

"Do as she says," the elder man said, the color having drained from his face.

"But—"

"Do it!" The youngest man's protest was cut off by the elder's shrill command. One after another, they picked up their guns, flung them overboard into the murky darkness of the water below. The loud splash each one made seemed to echo in the oppressive silence of the swamp.

Peyton watched as the last firearm disappeared into the water then turned her attention back to the poachers. "Now," she said in a cold voice that belied the fear worming through her gut, "let's talk about Tess Ballard."

Gritting his teeth, the young man looked down at his boots before saying, "Tess...she cheated on me. With my brother."

"And so you murdered her?" Peyton couldn't keep her disgust out of her voice.

"Murder?" The guy looked genuinely surprised. "Who said anything about murder?"

"But you said she had it coming..." Peyton recalled.

"Yeah, well...I was angry and drunk when I said that. I didn't mean she had to die, just that she deserved to get hurt for what she did. She had this boat – she was really proud of it; it was her daddy's – and so I took some lighter fluid and..." He shrugged. "I couldn't just let her treat me like that."

Peyton eyed him critically for a moment before letting out a sigh. Was he telling the truth? She had a hard time imagining him coming up with such a story on the spot.

"What about Jennifer Easton?" she asked.

The three men exchanged bewildered glances.

"Who?" the elder asked.

Peyton's heart sank. She was beginning to think this had all been a big waste of time.

"I told you I work for the National Park Service," she said. "My partner's out here somewhere, but I'm not sure where. Have you seen him, by any chance? His name's Sean O'Malley."

The burly man shook his head. "It's been just us three since we lit out...what...around noon?" He looked at his fellows, who nodded. "Thought we were the only ones in the area—until you showed up, that is."

Peyton was on the verge of deciding to cut her losses and leave, but just she thought of the island she and Sean had visited earlier, the one where they'd found Jennifer Easton's shoe prints and Patrick Sharma's library card. What had Chip called the island?

Île des Serpents Morts. The Island of the Dead Snakes.

"Have any of you heard of a place called the Island of the Dead Snakes?"

A strange look came over the faces of the men. The youngest paled, his bravado evaporating. The burly man clenched his jaw, eyeing Peyton warily, while the elder momentarily closed his eyes, as if praying.

"That's not a place you want to go," the elder finally said. His voice was hoarse, and he looked older in that moment than Peyton had initially estimated.

"Why not? What's there?" Peyton asked, her heart pounding in her chest.

"Death, mostly." The burly man's voice was gruff with disdain. "It's cursed."

"Cursed?" Peyton scoffed at that. "Are you serious?"

"Dead serious." The younger man looked up at her, fear apparent in his eyes. "That's where my cousin went...he ain't been seen since."

"What's your cousin's name?" Peyton asked.

"Patrick Sharma," he answered quietly.

Peyton nodded, lowering her weapon. "I'm investigating his death—his and three others. And I was at the island earlier today."

"That's probably why your partner's missing," the burly man muttered.

His voice was flat, devoid of any emotion. Peyton's blood ran cold.

"Why would you say that?" she demanded, her grip on the weapon tightening again.

The elder poacher, who had been silent for a while, now spoke up, his voice little more than a whisper. "There's a legend about Île des Serpents Morts. They say it's haunted by the spirits of those who've died there. Anyone who goes to the island never returns...at least not as they were."

Peyton stared at him, stunned into silence. She wasn't normally one to believe in ghost stories or legends, but the fear she saw reflected in the poacher's eyes was very real. It chilled her to the bone.

"You're saying my partner is...what? Dead?"

The burly man gave her a look that was almost pitying. "If he went to the island, yeah...that's probably what happened."

"No," Peyton said, shaking her head vehemently. "I went there, and I'm still alive."

They all stared back in silence. *And how much longer will that be the case?* their eyes seemed to say.

"Believe what you want," the youngest man said, sounding resigned and far older than his years. "Just don't go looking for him on that cursed island."

Peyton took a deep breath before sheathing her weapon. She looked each man in the eye before speaking again. "Actually, that's exactly where I need to go. And I need you to tell me how to get there."

The three men exchanged glances before the elder man finally let out a sigh and spoke, "It's due north of here. You'll see a tall cypress tree with an outgrowth in the shape of a serpent's head. That marks the entrance to the waterway that leads to Île des Serpents Morts."

Peyton nodded, memorizing the information. "Anything else I should know?"

The elder man looked at her for a long time before answering. "Keep your eyes up. Whatever you do...keep your eyes up."

Peyton wasn't really sure what to make of this comment, but she nodded anyway. "Thanks for the information."

She was about to dive into the water and swim back to the airboat she'd left in the weeds, but then it occurred to her that these poachers might come after her. There was something cold and unforgiving in the burly man's eyes, even if the other two showed no hostility at the moment. Better to make them swim back to her boat while she took theirs.

"You know what?" she said, a mischievous glint in her eye. "I think I'll take your boat."

The men's faces fell as they realized what she was implying.

"This is our livelihood," argued the burly man, his eyes narrowing dangerously at her. But Peyton wasn't about to back down.

"An *illegal* livelihood," she said. "I saw that gator you shot. Or, if you prefer, consider this payback for Tess Ballard. You set her boat on fire, and now I'm taking yours."

"Look, lady," he said, "we've been out here all day, and I think I speak for all of us when I say we're bone tired. How are we supposed to get back without a boat? Swim to shore?"

"No. My boat's back there in the woods." Peyton pointed. "You can return it to the nearest police station—the same place where you'll find your own boat waiting in the morning."

"You want us to swim to it?" the younger man asked, nervously eyeing the dark water.

"I did it. Afraid your gator friend will want revenge?"

The men didn't argue further. Perhaps it was the steely resolve in Peyton's eyes, the way she held herself, or maybe it was fear of the gun she still had holstered at her side. Whatever the reason, they dropped into the water one after the other, swimming for the barely visible outline of the airboat tied up securely among the reeds. Peyton watched as they disappeared into the darkness, their heads bobbing on the surface of the water, before turning her attention to their boat. It was a larger model than hers with a more powerful motor; it was clear that they had been investing heavily in their illegal activities.

A pang of satisfaction hit her. This could well put them out of business.

Climbing aboard, she took a final look at the desolate swamp around her. The moon hung low in the sky, illuminating the gnarled trees and murky water. The occasional splash and rustle in the undergrowth were the only signs of life. As eerie as it was, Peyton knew she would have to venture further into its depths to reach Île des Serpents Morts to find her partner, Sean.

As she steered the boat through a winding channel, she ruminated on what she'd been told about the island. The poachers' tale had been chilling, convincing even. Peyton didn't believe in curses or spirits...yet her mind nagged at her nonetheless. Every legend, after all, was founded on some piece of truth, wasn't it?

So what was the truth about the Island of Dead Snakes?

CHAPTER TWENTY TWO

When Peyton's eyes began to grow heavy, she told herself she would just let them rest for a few moments.

However, the silent darkness and the rhythmic hum of the boat's engine soon lulled her into a deeper sleep than she'd intended. When she woke up, it was with a start. Groggily, she tried to make sense of her surroundings.

The boat was lodged among tall reeds, and the air was thick with the musk of still water. Peyton's heart pounded in her chest as she realized she had drifted off course.

The only question remaining now was how far.

Pulling out the compass she'd found on the boat, she cursed under her breath as she saw the needle point due south, indicating that she had deviated significantly from her original path. She needed to correct her course.

First, however, she needed to get out of the reeds and back into the channel.

This was easier said than done. The reeds were thick and clawed at the sides of the boat, seemingly alive in their resistance. She engaged the engine, the mechanical hum shattering the eerie silence around her. Yet the boat didn't move.

Sighing heavily, Peyton grabbed a long, sturdy branch that had been stowed on the boat, presumably for such occasions. Using it as a pole, she pushed against the muddy swamp floor, forcing the boat back into motion.

"Come on," she muttered under her breath. "Work with me here."

She pushed again, and this time she managed to free the boat from its marshy prison. She wiped sweat from her brow and adjusted her compass, making sure to stay on course toward Île des Serpents Morts. The rhythmic churning of the engine rumbled through the silent swamp, disrupted only by the occasional unseen creature launching itself into the murky water.

Then, all at once, the engine began to cough and sputter. At first, Peyton suspected the reeds may have gotten caught in the engine somehow. But then she glanced at the fuel gauge and saw she was on empty.

Damn it! she thought as the engine died. Why hadn't she kept an eye on it?

"At least there's a spare gas can," she murmured, turning around and digging beneath a coil of rope for the can she'd seen earlier. There were two cans, actually, though one was already empty. The second one, fortunately, was full.

Peyton unscrewed the cap, then hefted the can. As she did so, a few drops splashed on her clothes. She took a few awkward steps toward the fuel tank before it occurred to her that she didn't smell gasoline.

Odd. Could it be some other type of fuel? She wasn't an expert on airboats by any stretch of the imagination, so it was simply a different kind of fuel.

A kind of fuel that had almost no scent.

Troubled, she set the can down, bent over it, and sniffed. Nothing. She dipped her finger in the liquid and, when she realized she still couldn't smell anything, she decided to taste it.

Water. It was water.

Her heart sank. Then, still trying to unscramble this mystery, she hurried over to the second can – the empty one – and unscrewed the cap. She immediately noticed the odor of gasoline.

They must've kept one for gas and one for water, she thought. *And they already used the last of the gas.*

It made sense. One of the poachers had claimed they'd already been out all day, and besides that, airboats weren't exactly fuel-efficient.

As the reality of the situation settled on Peyton, a thrill of fear ran through her. What would happen if she got stranded out here? Would her phone even work after being submerged in the water?

I'm stuck in the middle of a swamp at night, alone, and nobody even knows where I am.

Well, not entirely alone. The air around her buzzed with flying insects, and everywhere she turned, she thought she heard unseen creatures slipping through the water or rustling through the trees.

"Shit," she hissed under her breath. In the gloom, she fumbled to find her phone. It flickered on, and Peyton breathed a sigh of relief as she saw it had survived its earlier swim and was still operational. She dialed Sean's number but was met with no response. She considered calling Wilder, but then she recalled their last conversation. He had warned her about coming out here, after all. Besides, if he wasn't willing to search for Sean in the dark, why would he send a search party out for her?

Just then, as the boat continued to drift forward under its own momentum, she noticed a cypress tree with an odd outgrowth looming in front of her. It was twisted into a shape that bore a striking resemblance to a serpent's head, just as the elder poacher had described.

She had found the entrance to Île des Serpents Morts.

With a start, she searched the boat and was relieved to find a pair of oars, along with a flashlight. She picked up one of the oars and began to paddle, her strokes rough and unpracticed. The boat moved sluggishly, but it was better than nothing. As she moved closer to the island, the atmosphere seemed to change; it became silent and still as though the swamp creatures were holding their breath in anticipation.

A chill ran down her spine as she stepped onto the seemingly deserted island. The moonlight filtering through the dense foliage created an eerie tableau of shadows and silhouettes, playing tricks on her already strained nerves. She hadn't liked this place in the daylight, and it was even worse in the darkness.

If Sean was taken by the killer, she thought, *there's a good chance Sean ended up here, just like Jennifer Easton and Patrick Sharma.* Peyton wasn't entirely sure whether the other two victims, Ava King and Jacob Ramirez, had ever come to the island, but she had a feeling they had.

She didn't have to be superstitious to recognize that this island was in the middle of the murders. Whoever was doing the killings, this place was very special to them.

Peyton took a deep breath and flipped on the flashlight she'd found onboard the confiscated boat. The beam of light cut through the inky darkness, casting long, skeletal shadows from the trees. She began to move, her footsteps soft against the mossy ground. The forest was eerily still, with only the sounds of her own nervous breathing and the occasional owl hooting somewhere in the canopy.

As she ventured deeper into the island, she felt an increasing sense of unease. Was it her imagination, or did the air actually grow colder as she went farther? Did the shadows seem to shift slightly when she moved her light across them? Peyton shook off these thoughts, chiding herself for letting old ghost stories get to her.

She thought about the elder poacher's final comment to her: *Keep your eyes up.* Taking the advice literally, she began to scan the upper branches of the mangroves. That was when she noticed a tall structure on stilts, rather like a large tree house, standing among the mangled trees. Upon closer inspection, it appeared to be a rustic look-out point or watchtower of sorts, with wooden stairs spiraling up its trunk and a rickety balcony encircling the top.

Steeling her nerves, Peyton began to ascend the staircase, each step creaking under her weight. Her heart pounded loudly in her ears, and her flashlight flickered ominously as she made her way up. When she finally reached the top, she found herself in front of a closed door with a padlock on it. She considered shooting the padlock, but the idea of giving herself away made her uneasy. She would have to find another way to open it.

Where's a lock picking set when you need one? she thought.

Since picking the lock didn't seem to be an option, Peyton took a step back, eyeing the door and its surrounds. There had to be another way inside. She looked up at the roof of the tower, squinting in the dim light. It was a simple wooden structure with a few holes in the roof. With enough effort, she could potentially climb up and then drop down through one of the openings.

With nothing to lose, Peyton hoisted herself onto the balcony's railing and pulled herself up toward the roof. The old wood groaned under her weight, but she gritted her teeth and kept climbing until she reached the top.

Her fingers were raw and throbbing by the time she managed to pull herself onto the roof of the tower. She lay there for a moment, panting hard as she surveyed her surroundings. The view from atop was both beautiful and incredibly lonely; she could see a wide expanse of swamp stretching out in all directions, punctuated here and there with gnarled cypress trees and skeletal mangroves.

She crawled over to one of the holes in the roof and lowered herself into the small opening. It was tight; she barely managed to slip through, scraping her elbows and knees against rough splinters. As she landed inside, there was a sudden fluttering sound and something passed through the air close to her face. Then there was more rustling all around her, a growing sound that filled the confined space, and her flashlight picked up several dozen dark shapes darting around her.

Bats.

Trying not to panic, she covered her face and lowered her head as the cloud of bats swirled and swirled, whirling up and out of the other openings in the roof, their leathery bodies barely grazing her. Peyton held her breath, waiting for the chaos to end.

When the last bat had finally escaped, she straightened and dusted herself off. *Easy,* she told herself, trying to calm her breathing. *It's alright.*

Calm again, she shone her flashlight around the room. She gasped at what the light revealed: rows of precariously stacked books, grimy glass vials filled with mysterious liquids, aged maps of the swamp and the island, and most importantly, newspaper clippings about each of the murder victims.

"Ava, Patrick, Jacob," she muttered to herself as she skimmed over each neatly clipped article. There was nothing about Jennifer, but that was probably because of how recently she'd been killed.

It was clear now: Peyton was standing right in the monster's den.

Several dark stains on the wood caught her attention. Blood—she was sure of it. But it was old. There were feathers, too, which suggested to her that the blood was animal, perhaps from some kind of ritual sacrifices. She hoped it wasn't human.

A harsh wind blew outside, making the tower creak ominously. Fear gripped Peyton tighter than before as she realized how isolated she was, yet there was a morbid fascination that kept her going. She rummaged through stacks of notes filled with illegible handwriting and symbols that looked like some ancient language, several of which resembled the occultic symbol she and Sean had found carved into a tree on their previous visit to the island.

The thought of her partner jolted her back to reality. She wasn't here to satisfy her curiosity, but to find – and rescue, if necessary – her partner.

But where was he?

Glancing around, she noticed a window covered with a sheet of warped plywood. She pulled the plywood off, thinking she might be able to climb out the window and get back to the ground, but then she discovered a pair of ropes leading off to another tree a short distance away. One of the ropes was about six feet above the other, probably designed for someone to walk on the bottom rope while holding onto the top one.

But how old were these ropes? Would they hold her?

And more importantly, where did they lead?

Only one way to find out, she thought.

Firmly gripping her flashlight between her teeth, she reached out and tested the lower rope, finding it to be surprisingly sturdy. She cast a wary look at the dim, gloomy forest below—the height was dizzying, but she could not afford to surrender to fear now.

Gritting her teeth, Peyton placed one foot tentatively on the lower rope. With a firm grip on the top one, she began to edge along the primitive bridge, which swayed under her weight.

It seemed an eternity before she reached the opposite tree. The tree was huge, and it took Peyton a few moments to realize she recognized it.

It's the same tree Sean and I saw earlier, she thought. *The one near where we found Jennifer Easton's footprints.*

The massive cypress was ringed with strange symbols, just like the one she'd discovered in the tower. *What's going on here?* she wondered. *Is someone living on this island?*

She was still examining the marks when she heard the scream.

CHAPTER TWENTY THREE

It was a man's scream, a cry of anger and defiance, and the sound of it rolled through the darkness of the island, silencing the nocturnal creatures whose rustlings and movements Peyton had been hearing moments before.

Peyton glanced around desperately as she tried to locate the source of the sound. She saw something in the distance—a flashlight, perhaps. It winked on, then went out.

The clamor of the island was slowly returning; the nocturnal animals were now daring to make their presence known. But Peyton barely noticed. Her mind was wholly consumed by one thought: she had to get to Sean.

Just then, Peyton noticed another pair of ropes leading from the giant cypress to an adjacent tree. How many ropes were up here, how many pathways for someone to move silently through the trees? She didn't know, and at the moment she didn't particularly care.

She worked her way through the branches to the next pair of ropes. Then, holding onto the top one and stepping onto the bottom one, she began to walk across the treacherous bridge toward the next tree.

The wind picked up, nudging her. The rain was starting again, and the air was cooler now, causing her to shiver. She'd expected humidity and heat when she came to Louisiana—not to wish she'd dressed more warmly.

She was halfway across the rope when it snapped beneath her. Peyton screamed as she flung her hands upwards, gripping onto the top rope as her legs dangled in the air. She could taste the salty fear on her lips, feel every shiver of the gusty wind slapping against her cheeks. For a few dangerously long seconds, she swayed there precariously, desperately clutching onto the lifeline.

She briefly considered climbing back, but discarded the thought almost instantly. Sean needed her. Breathing heavily, she began moving forward, hand over hand, almost like she was back on the playground as a kid working the monkey bars.

Her muscles protested with every move, but she ignored the pain and forced herself onwards. Every inch felt like miles as she fought gravity and fatigue. Shadows danced below her, the wind whistling in her ears, trying to shake her down. But she held on.

Finally, after what felt like an eternity of struggle, she reached the next tree. She dragged herself onto one of its sturdy branches, chest heaving as she gulped down air.

As she looked around, deciding where to go next, there was a flash of lightning. In that second of illumination, she discovered she was nearly at the edge of the swamp. She could see a vast expanse of dark water spread out like a hand, its fingers poking between wooded islands. Closer, a rope tied to a branch of the very tree Peyton was in dangled over the water.

A man was swinging from that rope, his hands clutching at the noose around his neck.

Sean!

Her heart froze and shattered into a thousand pieces. *No, no, no!* her mind screamed. It couldn't be. But the next flash of lightning cemented the grim reality.

It was Sean alright, swinging like a helpless marionette from the gnarled branch. His eyes bulged in terror, and his legs kicked feebly as he dangled above the water.

Peyton could hear her own screams now, filling the night air. The world had become a chaotic flurry of wind and rain and terror. An animalistic sound rumbled through her chest – grief, fear, rage – she couldn't tell anymore.

But there was no time to mourn. She forced herself to move, scrambling along the branch toward Sean, praying that she was not too late. His struggles were growing weaker, his movements slower, the jerking spasms of a man fighting for his last breath.

When Peyton reached the place where the rope was tied to the branch, she pulled out her knife and started sawing, using all the strength she could muster. The rope was thick, aged, and stubborn. The knife seemed woefully inadequate for the task.

Overhead, lightning streaked across the sky again, casting sickly shadows on Sean's face. His eyes were rolling back, his body twisting and convulsing in a grotesque dance of death.

"No, no," Peyton muttered under her breath as she sawed furiously at the rope above Sean. It was fraying, but not quickly enough. She wished she had an ax or a chainsaw, anything more powerful than the little knife she was working with.

Rain began to fall harder, saturating her, obscuring her vision. But

Peyton didn't care about the rain or the cold wind biting at her skin. She could only focus on Sean.

"Please," she whispered to the knife, to the rope, to the universe itself. "Please."

Finally, with a sound that was almost a sigh of relief, the rope gave way under her relentless sawing. It snapped clean, releasing Sean, who tumbled into the murky water below.

Without sparing another thought, Peyton launched herself off the tree, plunging into the darkness below after him. The water hit hard against her skin, stealing her breath away. It was murky and cool, a dark abyss swallowing her whole. But she forced herself down, fingers straining in the void as she sought out Sean.

She hit something solid—Sean. She wrapped her arms around him and kicked upwards, jaw clenched against the icy water that seeped past her lips. She could feel his limp body bobbing helplessly against her efforts, his heartbeat faint under her hands.

Bursting to the surface, she gasped for air, hauling Sean's head above the waterline. The rain pounded on them mercilessly, obscuring her vision and making it hard to breathe.

But Peyton pushed on, struggling to keep their heads above water. With one arm tightly wrapped around Sean's chest and the other thrashing against the water in a desperate attempt to swim, she kicked and floundered toward the shore.

Between them and the solid ground of the island lay a morass of mud and marshy vegetation, a challenging terrain to navigate even on a good day. Peyton's heart pounded in her chest as she squinted through the relentless downpour, trying to find an easier way ashore.

But none presented itself. There was nothing but dense undergrowth and clinging mud in front of her. It was the stuff of nightmares, and it was the only thing standing between them and safety.

Gritting her teeth, Peyton plunged into the swamp. The mud sucked at their bodies like hands trying to pull them down. Every step was a battle against the elements. Cold, wet, and desperate, she dragged Sean's unresponsive form toward what looked like a small clearing ahead.

As they neared the shore, Sean's weight seemed to increase exponentially with every labored step she took. Peyton's muscles trembled under the strain, her body screaming for mercy as she fought against the pull of the merciless mud below them. The last few feet were sheer torment, but she didn't dare stop.

Finally, with one last desperate lunge, Peyton managed to drag Sean onto solid ground. Exhaustion gnawed at her limbs, and each breath came in jagged gasps.

"Sean! Sean!" She shook him gently. His clothes were soaked and heavy from the rain and swamp water; his skin was cool under her touch.

She pressed two fingers against his wrist, feeling for a pulse. It was weak and irregular, but it was there. Peyton let out a shaky breath she didn't realize she'd been holding, relief washing over her like a warm tide. But that relief was fleeting as the gravity of their situation rushed back.

Sean needed medical attention. Fast. He had been hanging from that rope for too long, his body subjected to a cruel dance of life and death. His pulse was weak, erratic, and his complexion ghostly pale under the harsh light of the storm.

"Peyton," he murmured, his voice a ragged whisper carried by the relentless wind. His eyes fluttered open, unfocused as they searched for her.

"I'm here," Peyton said, grabbing his clammy hand and squeezing it tightly. "You're going to be okay." She wasn't sure if that was a promise she could keep, but she knew he needed to hear it.

They weren't out of danger yet. They were stranded in the middle of a swamp during a vicious storm with little more than her willpower. Peyton glanced up at the merciless sky that thrashed them with rain and wind, steeling herself against the daunting task ahead.

She had to get Sean out of this hellhole alive. She would not let this wet deathbed become his tomb.

"Peyton," he said again.

"Shh. Don't speak. I'm going to get us out of here." She pulled out her phone, desperately hoping it would still work despite being submerged in water multiple times. To her relief, the screen lit up. She had never been so grateful for modern technology in all her life.

Peyton dialed Officer Wilder's number. He might not know how to reach the island, but Chip should, so if only Wilder could locate Chip—

Sean, grimacing with the effort, raised his hand and pointed one finger, directing Peyton's attention to something behind her. At the same time, she heard a cold voice she didn't recognize say, "Put the phone down, or you're both dead."

117

CHAPTER TWENTY FOUR

Peyton froze. The phone was still ringing, and a moment later she heard Wilder speaking from it. "Hello? Hello? Who is this?"

"If you answer him," the man behind Peyton said, "I will jab this knife between your shoulder blades."

Without turning around, Peyton slowly lowered the phone to the ground, her heartbeat echoing loudly in her ears. Her fingers trembled, but she made sure to place the device gently on the muddy ground, not wanting to draw attention to herself.

"Turn it off," the voice commanded.

Peyton hesitated. She wanted desperately to tell Wilder what was going on, but even if she did so, it would take hours for help to find them, and by then it might be too late. No, it was better to keep the man behind her from doing anything rash.

She ended the call.

"Smart," the voice said, a hint of approval in its cold tone. "Now, stand up slowly, keeping your hands where I can see them."

Peyton obeyed, her legs shaking as she pushed herself upright. She could feel the man's presence behind her, the threat of the knife against her back a silent reminder of her vulnerability.

"Who are you?" she asked, her voice barely above a whisper. She didn't expect an answer, but the question seemed to fill the heavy silence between them.

"That's not important, is it?" the man said, ignoring her question. His voice was closer now, and Peyton could feel his breath on her neck. Something sharp touched her back, just to the side of her spine, and then she felt her gun yanked from the holster. The knife moved away as the man stepped back.

"Does anyone know where you are?" the man asked.

Peyton thought back to her last conversation with Wilder, the argument during which she had tried to convince him to go into the swamps with her and search for Sean. Wilder had insisted it was too dangerous, but in the end he had helped Peyton by giving her directions—that, and not stopping her from stealing an airboat.

Wilder had known Peyton was going to this island. But did she dare reveal that information? Or was it better to lie?

"No, I'm alone. I came here by myself," Peyton said, trying to keep her voice steady.

"Let's hope that's true. We wouldn't want anyone else getting hurt, now would we?" the man said, a cold edge to his voice.

Peyton risked a glance over her shoulder, trying to catch a glimpse of their captor. All she could see was a dark figure, rain dripping off a hooded slicker. He stepped back, the knife now concealed in the shadows.

"Now, I'm going to need you to turn around and walk toward the water. If you try anything, I won't hesitate to use this knife," he said, gesturing with the weapon.

Peyton turned slowly, her mind racing. She needed to think of a plan, a way to disarm him or create a distraction. But her body was exhausted, her limbs trembling with fatigue. She wasn't sure she had the strength to fight.

"What about Sean?" she said. "He needs medical attention. At the very least, he needs to get out of this rain."

A few seconds passed in silence. Then the man said, "Sean? Can you hear me?"

Sean didn't answer.

"If you don't answer me," the man said, "I'm going to hurt your friend here."

Still, there was no answer.

"I'm telling you," Peyton said, "he probably went into shock. He can't—"

The man advanced toward her in two long strides and struck her hard across the cheek. She cried out and fell back into the mud.

"Let's try this again," the man said. "Can you hear me now, Sean?"

Sean's voice was low, exhausted. "Yes."

"Good. I need you to get up—the three of us are going for a little trip. I'd say we could cut across the island, but given your state, it's probably better to go by water. I've got a boat just a short distance down the shore. You can either go to that boat or die here—your choice."

Peyton looked at Sean, worry etched on her face. She knew he was in no condition to travel, but what choice did they have? The man's threat was clear.

"Okay," she said, her voice shaking. "We'll go with you."

She pushed herself up from the mud, wincing as her bruised

cheekbone protested. The man watched her, the gun still in his hand.

"Let's go," he said, gesturing with the gun toward the shore.

Peyton helped Sean to his feet, supporting most of his weight as they stumbled along the shore. The man followed close behind, the gun still poised and ready. Peyton stole a glance at him, but she couldn't see much other than the outline of his towering figure in the rain-soaked darkness. His face remained obscured beneath the low brim of his hat.

She focused on each painful step through the chilling rain and mud, a terrible possibility gnawing at her mind: Perhaps she and Sean were being led to their demise, in a lonely corner of this godforsaken island. The fear enveloped her, as chilling as the rain that soaked her bones.

"Why are you doing this?" she asked.

"For the same reason I killed the others. This island is sacred, and you've trespassed on it. There are consequences."

"That's bullshit," Peyton snapped, her fear momentarily overshadowed by a surge of anger. "The people you killed were innocent. They didn't deserve to die just because they happened upon this particular patch of mud."

"It's not just a patch of mud." The man's voice was a low growl. "This island is a place of power, a remnant from an ancient civilization that you uncultured swine couldn't possibly comprehend. The secrets it holds...the knowledge...it's meant for the chosen ones, not for outsiders."

Peyton could hear the fanaticism in his voice, the fervor of a man who truly believed he was doing some higher duty. It made him more dangerous, but also potentially gave her an angle to exploit. She just had to figure out how.

"What if we could respect your island?" Peyton said. "We could leave, never come back. And we wouldn't tell anyone about this place."

The man laughed, a harsh sound that echoed off the trees around them. "Nice try. No, as soon as you got back, you'd have boatloads of your friends combing this island for me."

Dogs, too, Peyton thought.

Sean stumbled, and Peyton caught him. She didn't know what devious plan their captor had in mind for when they reached the boat, but she did know their best bet was to turn the tables on him before they reached the boat. She thought about her earlier confrontation with the poachers, and how one of them had remarked that her gun might not fire because it was waterlogged. Peyton hadn't been forced to test the man's theory...but what if he'd been right?

What if the gun pointed at her right now was as useless as a chunk of wood? Was *she* willing to test that theory?

Without a concrete plan, she knew it was a gamble. Then again, the way things were looking, a long shot seemed to be their only shot. With her heart pounding in her chest, Peyton steeled herself.

The path to the boat was much farther than the man had let on. The rain-slicked shore made each step treacherous and slow. All she needed was the right moment—a moment of distraction.

Then, suddenly, there was a rustling in the grass to their right. She caught sight of a gator's retreating tail, and, knowing the man probably had turned in that direction, Peyton lunged.

Using all her remaining strength, she slammed into the man's side, knocking him off balance. He stumbled, releasing a surprised grunt. She reached for the gun, pushing it aside just as he pulled the trigger.

The gunshot exploded beside her ear, deafening her. She recoiled, her ears ringing, and the man clubbed her hard across the head. She fell back, stumbling into Sean and tumbling to the ground on top of him. His breath went out in a harsh wheeze, and she rolled off him, her vision swirling.

"Sean?" she asked, blinking through the pain that throbbed in her head. "Are you okay?"

"Enough!" the man shouted, pointing the gun at them. He was furious, his nostrils flaring and his jaw clenching, and for a few heart-pounding moments Peyton thought he would end it here and now, regardless of what devious plot he'd intended to carry out. All it took was one look to see that he was capable of such summary violence.

Then, gradually, he lowered the weapon. His face grew composed, almost mischievous. "No," he said, "that would be too good for you— too easy. We're going to do this the right way. That doesn't mean, though, that I need you to be in one piece. If you try something like that again..." He shrugged. "Well, we might just have to see how well you can make do with a shattered kneecap."

Peyton knew better than to call his bluff. If she tested him again, he would carry out his threat—of that she had no doubt.

"What's your 'right way,' then?" Sean managed to ask, his breathing heavy. "You said there was a right way."

The man's smile was cold and calculating. "I could tell you...but that would spoil the fun, wouldn't it?" His smile faded. "Now *walk*."

Peyton rose and helped Sean to his feet, and then they resumed their journey in silence, the rain beating down on them relentlessly. The man remained several paces behind Peyton and Sean, close enough to keep track of them but far enough away to rob Peyton of any chance of wrestling the gun from him. Had Peyton been alone, she might have looked for an opportunity to make a run for it, losing herself in the brush while the man was distracted with the cry of a bird starting up from the grass or the splash of a gator slipping into water.

But she knew that doing so would be a death sentence for Sean. She couldn't abandon him, not when he needed her most, not even to save her own life.

This is what it means to be partners, she thought grimly. *It's like marriage: You're in it through thick and thin, no matter the challenges you're up against.*

She nodded to herself, content with this resolution. If she had to die, at least she and Sean would die together.

She was still thinking about this when they came upon a dilapidated wooden dock that jutted out into the swamp. A small airboat was tethered to it, and behind it an ever smaller dinghy.

And coiled in the airboat, one end dangling over the side like a serpent's tail, was a vine.

CHAPTER TWENTY FIVE

"Get in," the man commanded, gesturing toward the boat with his gun.

Peyton, her mind working feverishly to come up with a plan, led Sean toward the dinghy, supporting him.

"Not him," the man said. "He's coming with me in the airboat. You get in the dinghy by yourself."

Peyton stared at the man, desperately trying to predict what he was planning. All four of the victims had been strangled to death. Was he going to kill her the same way?

As if reading her thoughts, the man walked over to the airboat, reached down, and picked up the vine. He tossed her one end of the vine, and Peyton caught it. The vine was already tied into a noose.

"Put that around your neck," he said.

Peyton's blood went cold. *This must be how he killed the others,* she thought. *He put them in a boat and drove ahead of them, pulling them along like a dog on a leash—and strangling them in the process.*

And now he was going to do it to her if she didn't think of a way out of the situation. But what could she do? The man had a gun, and Sean couldn't exactly help. He was pretty much sleepwalking at this point. Anything Peyton tried would not only endanger herself but Sean as well. She had to be smart.

And careful.

"Peyton, don't do it," Sean rasped, his voice hoarse and filled with despair. But she silenced him with a look.

The man was watching her closely, a gleeful anticipation in his eyes, and Peyton took the opportunity to study him closely for the first time. He was tall, with a lean build and a weathered face that spoke of years spent under the sun. His eyes were a striking cobalt blue, cold and emotionless as they focused on her. A scar ran down the side of his face, interrupting the rough stubble on his cheek and giving him a menacing appearance.

He was almost smiling.

He's enjoying holding this power over us, Peyton thought. It made her sick.

Taking a deep breath, Peyton took the end of the vine, studying it. It was rough and scratchy against her skin, and its greenish-brown hue blended in with the existing foliage that surrounded them on all sides; nature's cruel camouflage.

"Is this part of your sacred ritual?" she asked, wrapping the vine around her palm as if to check its strength. She wanted him talking, wanted him distracted.

He raised an eyebrow at her but indulged her curiosity. "Yes," he said. "A cleansing ceremony of sorts. You see, the ancient civilization that once inhabited this island believed in purging the world of impurities."

Peyton didn't respond but kept her gaze fixed on the man, feigning interest. She had to maintain the illusion that she was compliant while secretly formulating a plan to turn the tables on him.

"And you believe you have the authority to carry out this cleansing?" she asked hesitantly, playing into his delusions.

His chest swelled with pride as he answered. "I am the chosen one, bestowed with the knowledge and responsibility to protect this sacred land. The power it holds flows through me."

Peyton nodded, slowly unwinding the vine from her palm. "So, what happens after these impurities are purged?"

A hint of a smile crossed his lips. "Once they are eliminated, the island will be able to flourish as it was intended. It will reveal its secrets only to those who are worthy."

"I see," Peyton said, her voice dripping with feigned admiration. "And how do you determine who is worthy?"

The man's eyes gleamed with fervor as he stepped closer, his grip on the gun tightening. "The island speaks to me," he said, his voice barely above a whisper. "It reveals its secrets only to those who have proven their loyalty and dedication."

Now! she thought. *Just give him a shove, and he'll fall into the swamp!*

Her muscles tensed. He might be able to get one shot off before she reached him, but even if the bullet hit her, she could survive a single bullet wound, couldn't she? All she would have to do is staunch the bleeding and wait…

Wait for what? For Wilder to change his mind and decide it was worthwhile to come searching for them even in the dark? No, she couldn't put all her eggs in that basket. Waiting for help was far too uncertain a plan.

She needed to grab the airboat and get the hell out of this swamp.

But how do I get Sean into the boat with me without either of us getting shot?

The man was watching her closely. The lightning flickered, and she got a better look at him. He was tall and wiry, with greasy hair that clung to his forehead and bloodshot eyes. There was no doubt in her mind that he would kill them without hesitation if he sensed any sign of resistance.

How did you become such a fanatic? she wondered. *Who were you before all this?*

"How did you first come to this island?" she asked.

The man grinned knowingly and wagged a finger at her. "You're stalling. It won't do you any good. You can feign interest all you like, but I know what you really are."

"And what's that?" she asked.

"A parasite," he sneered. "Like the others before you. An intruder, trying to strip this place of its power."

Peyton's heart raced as she carefully edged closer to him, keeping her movements slow and deliberate. She had to keep him talking, keep him distracted. If she could just get within striking distance…

"I assure you, I have no interest in taking anything from this island," she said, trying to sound sincere. "I simply want to understand it. To learn from its secrets."

"Enough!" the man said, raising the weapon. "Get in the boat, or I'll shoot you."

Still, Peyton hesitated, ready to spring. If she got into that boat, she was dead—she felt certain of that. But if she lunged at him, if she managed to shove him into the water…

"Alright, then," the man said. He pointed the gun at Sean. "I'll shoot your partner instead."

"No!" Peyton said immediately, taking a step back and raising her hands. "Okay, I'll get in the boat." Without waiting for a response, she climbed into the dinghy. She sat down, the vine still around her throat, feeling as helpless as a lamb led to slaughter. If the man, who was still holding the other end of the vine, got into the airboat and started forward, the noose around Peyton's neck would tighten, choking her.

And then what would happen? Once it was over, would Sean suffer the same fate?

With a smug smile, the man pushed Sean toward the airboat. Sean stumbled, barely keeping from falling. He caught himself on the edge of the boat and glanced in Peyton's direction, and it looked almost as if he...what...winked? Had he really winked at her? Did Sean have a plan she didn't know about?

Peyton watched in tense anticipation as Sean climbed into the airboat, followed by the man with the gun. He tied the end of the vine to the frame of the airboat, then started the engine.

"Hold on tight!" he called over his shoulder to Peyton, his voice merry. "We wouldn't want to lose you, would we?"

CHAPTER TWENTY SIX

As the airboat pulled forward, the man picked up the slack in the vine, presumably so that it wouldn't get caught up in any weeds. Peyton tried to slip the noose off her neck, but as she reached for it, the man gave the vine a sharp tug, tightening the noose.

"Uh-uh-uh!" he said. "Can't have you getting loose!"

He laughed at his own joke as Peyton's hands dropped to her lap.

That's what this all is to him, she thought disconsolately. *A big joke.*

But no, that wasn't true, was it? This man was a true believer. He believed he was protecting the island, maybe even avenging it. And Peyton and Sean were just the means to a personal end for him.

Peyton glanced at Sean, who was now sitting opposite the man. His eyes were downcast, his body somnolent as if still in that sleepwalker-like state. Yet he *had* winked, hadn't he? Or was that just a figment of her panicked imagination?

Please have a plan, Sean. Please have a plan.

The airboat picked up speed, leading them deeper into the heart of the swamp. The vine around Peyton's neck pulled tighter and tighter. She found herself gasping for breath, clutching at the coarse, relentless vine, trying to take the pressure off her throat.

She could feel the breath being squeezed out of her, the edges of her vision starting to blur. Despite her initial strength, she was starting to weaken, her hands struggling to loosen the vine around her neck.

"Sean!" She tried to yell through a constricted throat, but all that came out was a strangled sound. She looked toward him, pleading with her eyes.

Whatever you're planning, Sean, you'd better do it now! she tried to tell him with her eyes. *I can't wait any longer!*

Then, just when she was beginning to resign herself to the idea that she had misread Sean, she noticed that his hand was dangling over the side of the boat. He was holding out three fingers, and she watched, he retracted one of the fingers into his fist, leaving two.

He pulled back another finger, leaving only his pointer sticking out.

Then, with a speed that surprised Peyton, he lunged toward the man. The man spun, as if he had known all along that Sean might be

127

stronger than he was pretending, but before he could fire, Peyton threw herself to the side, causing the other end of the vine to bump into the man's legs. It was just enough to cause him to stumble, firing into the bottom of the airboat instead of into Sean.

Then Sean crashed into the man, sending them both sprawling back onto the floor of the airboat. The weapon slid out of the man's grasp, skittering across the floor and coming to rest against a seat.

Peyton gasped for breath, clinging to the dinghy so that she wouldn't be dragged into the water by the vine. Her vision was darkening. She thought of the knife in her pocket, but she knew that if she let go of the boat even for a moment, the vine would pull her over the side.

Meanwhile, Sean and the man grappled on the floor, locked in a struggle for control. Sean managed to land a blow to the man's jaw that temporarily stunned him. Sean took advantage of his momentary confusion and pushed away, lunging for the abandoned weapon.

Before Sean could reach the weapon, however, the man grabbed the throttle and shoved it forward. Sean tumbled, the gun slipping from his grasp–

And that was all Peyton saw, because she lost her grip on the dinghy and went plunging into the water.

Darkness clouded Peyton's vision. She was being dragged through the swamp by the vine, her hands clawing at it but making no progress in freeing herself. Panic and fear welled up inside her.

Then she remembered the knife.

Now that she was in the water, she no longer had to worry about clinging to the boat. Keeping one hand on the vine, she used her other hand to dig around in her pocket for the knife, hoping she hadn't lost it in the struggle. Her fingers grazed the cool metallic handle, and a surge of relief washed over her. Peyton drew the blade and started hacking at the vine that was strangling her.

Water and debris filled her mouth as she struggled to cut the vine off. She felt the water around her churn, felt the cold seep into her bones. But she kept cutting, kept fighting, refusing to give up until finally, finally, the vine gave way.

The noose loosened around her neck, and for a moment everything was lightness, freedom. But only for a moment. Then she realized she was sinking into the murky depths of the swamp without anything to keep her afloat. Her heart seized in panic as she flailed against the dense water, but it was like trying to move through molasses. Her lungs screamed for air, but all she inhaled was darkness.

Just when she thought it might be over, Peyton felt a powerful grip around her wrist. She was pulled upwards, through the swampy murk. Gasping and choking, she broke the surface of the water.

Sean hauled her onto the damaged airboat, which sat partially submerged but still floating in the fetid swamp water. His face was pale, a stark contrast to his drenched clothing. There was a wild light in his eyes, a mixture of fear and relief that mirrored her own feelings.

Coughing and sputtering, she twisted away from him to throw up into the water. The taste of bile and swamp water lingered in her mouth.

"You alright?" Sean asked, his voice rough.

Peyton nodded, dragging herself upright. Her heart was still hammering in her chest, but she was alive. She looked at Sean with gratitude shining in her eyes.

She tried to thank him, but all that came out was a watery croak. She cleared her throat, coughed several times, and then asked, "Where is he?"

Sean didn't answer immediately. He was looking past her, his gaze hard and unwavering. Following his stare, Peyton turned to look over her shoulder.

The man was several feet away, tangled in the swampy undergrowth. The airboat had apparently crashed into a particularly aggressive bunch of stumps and roots, causing the man to be thrown out. Now he was lying still, the weeds creeping up his legs like the tentacles of some hideous sea monster.

"He's not a problem anymore," Sean said. His voice sounded tired but also relieved.

"Dead?" Peyton asked, her voice as thin as a reed.

"He hasn't moved," Sean said. "But I think he's alive."

"Then we'd better get him. We can't leave him out here, even if that's exactly what he deserves."

Sean turned to look at Peyton, his eyebrows raised in surprise. "You want to save him? After what he did?"

"We can't stoop to his level, Sean," she said, her voice shaky but firm. "We'll take him with us, let the authorities deal with him."

Sean gave her a long look, as if assessing whether she was in the right state of mind, then nodded. "You're right. It's not our call to make."

They turned the airboat around and headed back toward the man.

As they approached, it became clear that he was unconscious but breathing. Blood trickled from a scrape on his forehead, the scarlet droplets stark against his pallid skin. Peyton swallowed hard; this was their captor, their antagonist, now helpless and injured.

With Sean's help, she managed to haul the man into the boat. He moaned but didn't wake up. Peyton tried not to look at him; instead, she focused on Sean.

"How are you feeling?" she asked. "Tell me you weren't faking it all along."

"Faking?" He shook his head. "I was nearly strangled to death, same as you. But afterward, when *he* showed up..." He paused and swallowed. "I might've led him on a bit. Wanted him to think I was weak, unable to fight back."

"Well, it worked. Thank you for saving my life."

"You saved mine first."

Peyton stared into her partner's eyes. She felt a bond forming between them, the kind of bond that can only be forged in the fires of adversity, and she knew that this connection with Sean was special, something she might never share with another human being in her lifetime.

They had saved one another's lives, after all. That sort of thing didn't happen every day.

Sean frowned, his eyes serious as he gazed down at their prisoner. "We've got to tie him up. It's going to take hours to get back to the precinct, and I'm not going to spend that time waiting for him to jump us."

"I don't see any rope around."

Sean's gaze moved around the boat, finally settling on a length of the vine that Peyton had earlier hacked away from her neck. "We could use this," he suggested, holding it up.

Peyton felt chills run down her spine at the sight of the vine. Yet she knew they had no other choice. They had to immobilize Elliot before he woke up and tried to harm them again. So, swallowing her reservations, she nodded.

Together, they twisted the vine around Elliot's wrists and ankles, tying him up as securely as they could. As they worked, Peyton found herself glancing at Sean every now and then. Despite everything they'd been through – the danger, the fear, the violence – he was still there with her, steady and reliable. His presence was a comfort she hadn't realized she'd needed until now. She wondered if he felt the same way.

Once the restraints were secure, they laid Elliot on his back at the edge of the boat, away from the water pooling at the bottom where a bullet had punctured the hull.

"That should do it," Sean said. He paused, staring down at the unconscious man.

"Did he move?" Peyton asked.

"No. I was just thinking that this man murdered four people and almost killed us as well, all to protect his 'sacred' island, and we don't even know his name."

"He might have a wallet."

Sean looked at her for a moment, then nodded. He bent down and began to rummage through the man's pockets. After a few seconds, he pulled out a worn leather wallet. Inside was a driver's license, a few crumpled bills, and some faded photos. The man's name, according to the license, was Elliot Foster. His face seemed softer in the driver's license photo, less rugged and more human. But that didn't change the fact that this face belonged to a killer.

Peyton looked at the photos. Elliot was laughing in one of them, surrounded by people who were probably his friends or family. Seeing his joy, his normalcy before whatever twisted him into this monster, haunted Peyton.

"Elliot Foster," Sean said quietly as if trying to align the name with their experiences but finding it hard. "Didn't seem like an Elliot."

"Doesn't matter what his name is," Peyton murmured, her gaze gravitating back toward the unconscious man. "It doesn't change anything."

Sean nodded slowly, replacing the wallet in Elliot's pocket. "That's enough investigative work for now," he said. "Let's get the hell out of here."

He grabbed hold of the tiller and steered the damaged airboat away from the malevolent isle, leaving its secrets squirming in the murk. Peyton watched as the dense canopy of trees receded into the distance. The swamp, which had been their prison for what felt like ages, was now just a whisper on the horizon.

Peyton looked down at their captive. Elliot Foster. He seemed so incongruous lying there bound by vines on the bottom of their boat, his face pale and peaceful despite the pandemonium that he had orchestrated not too long ago. The weight of what they'd been through settled heavily on her shoulders.

"I'm going to call it in," she said after a while, her voice raw.

131

"Wilder needs to know." She reached for her phone, but she couldn't find it. She must've lost it earlier, perhaps while she was in the swamp.

"Ah, well," Sean said, not sounding particularly disappointed. "I guess we'll just have to surprise him when we get there, won't we?"

Peyton sank back in her seat, finally allowing herself to feel everything her body was telling her: every last ache, bruise, and cut. She wanted to curl into a ball and weep, but she held those emotions at bay, knowing it wasn't quite time to let everything out, not while she was still keeping an eye on a serial killer.

The rain had stopped some time ago, and now the clouds were breaking. Dawn was coming—Peyton could see the first golden shafts of sunlight piercing the sky, promising a new day not colored by fear and violence. Even though her body was on the brink of exhaustion, the anticipation of the sunrise filled her with a sense of hope, a renewal.

"Look at that," she said softly, pointing out the sky to Sean. His glance followed her finger, taking in the morning's light with a tired nod. "We've made it through, Sean."

"Yeah," he replied, his voice rough from the night's ordeal. "We sure did." They shared a silence then, as if allowing the truth of their survival to sink into their battered bodies and minds.

The airboat hummed beneath them as they skimmed over the murky waters toward civilization. Peyton found herself still fixated on Elliot Foster, her mind replaying their interactions over and over. She had been so close to dying that she could feel Death's cold breath against her neck. But instead of cowering under its shadow, she had fought back and survived.

She hadn't done so alone, however. She and Sean had worked as a team, putting their very lives in one another's hands. That was not something she took lightly.

As the light continued to grow and the island receded into the murky distance behind them, Peyton felt a surge of gratitude just to be alive. Each breath, painful as it was against her raw throat, was precious to her.

And she vowed never to take her life for granted again.

CHAPTER TWENTY SEVEN

Peyton, drifting in and out of a formless dream, felt a hand on her arm and recoiled, giving a startled cry. She raised her hands in self-defense, her chest heaving with each breath.

"Easy," Sean said, holding up both hands in a calming gesture. "It's just me."

Slowly, Peyton lowered her fists. Her heart was hammering against her ribcage as if seeking an escape. She glanced around to see that Sean had docked the airboat beside the precinct. The killer – Elliot Foster – still lay where she had last seen him, his hands bound together with the vine, his mouth open and drool oozing down his cheek.

"I'll be damned," a voice said, and Peyton turned to see Officer Wilder approaching, a look of startled bewilderment on his face. "I never thought I'd see the two of you alive again." His gaze flicked to Foster. "And who's this?"

"The source of all the trouble," Sean said, rubbing at his throat, which was still bruised from where the noose had choked him earlier.

Peyton straightened and wiped the sweat from her brow. She glanced at Sean, their eyes meeting for a brief moment before he turned back to Wilder, his face stoic. What was that she'd seen in Sean's eyes? Respect? Admiration?

Wilder parked his hands on his hips. "I think I'd better hear it all from the beginning."

Peyton opened her mouth, then closed it again. She thought of everything she and Sean had been through, all the dangers and surprises, and realized that even if she spent an hour trying to explain it to Wilder, she could never really convey what she'd experienced. Only Sean could understand because he'd been through a similar ordeal himself.

"There'll be time for that later," Sean said. "For now, the man needs medical attention—he was thrown from the airboat, and there's no telling what injuries he suffered. Peyton's pretty banged up, too, even if she won't admit it."

Peyton raised an eyebrow at him as if to say, *What about what you've been through?* Before her tired brain could formulate the words, however, Wilder spoke.

"Let's get you all inside then," he said. "I'm sure you could all use some dry clothes."

"And a hot drink," Peyton said.

With the help of Wilder and several of his officers, they carted Elliot Foster into the precinct, leaving behind the swamp and its deadly secrets. Peyton couldn't shake the feeling that she was standing on solid ground for the first time in days.

Peyton glanced back at the scrappy airboat that had carried them through so much. It was a battered and bruised vessel, which was exactly how she felt at the moment. But its engine still purred, and its fan still turned, and that was proof enough to her that they had survived.

"There's coffee, tea, snacks, whatever you need," Wilder said. "One of my boys has medical training—I'll send him in. There are blankets in that cabinet if you need them." He pointed.

"Thanks," Peyton said.

"I should be thanking you," Wilder said, looking a bit sheepish. "Earlier, when you wanted to go looking for Sean—"

"It's okay," Peyton said, waving it away with her hand. "Don't worry about it. All's well that ends well."

Wilder nodded, looking grateful. "Well, just know we're all grateful for the work you two did tonight, and the risks you took. And I'm sure the families of the victims will be plenty grateful, too."

Peyton and Sean both nodded. Wilder stood there a moment longer, as if trying to think of something more to say, and then ducked his head and left.

The room fell silent. Peyton found herself staring off into space, her eyes too tired to focus.

Suddenly, she felt a hand on her shoulder, a gentle weight that made her heart pound in an altogether different way than before. She turned to find Sean standing next to her, his gaze soft but intense.

"You okay?" he asked.

Peyton gave a small, dry laugh. "Do I look like it?" she retorted lightly, trying to shake off the lingering dread and exhaustion.

Sean chuckled, dropping his hand and backing away a bit. "Well, you've looked better." His eyes, however, held nothing but admiration and respect for her.

A dull knock on the door interrupted them. A young officer walked in carrying a medical kit. He gave them an awkward salute before setting to work on their various injuries. Peyton found herself gritting her teeth as the disinfectant touched raw skin, and Sean winced slightly when his bruised throat was checked.

Once they were patched up, Sean rose and fetched two mugs of hot coffee for them from the countertop. Handing one to Peyton, he said, "Here's to surviving." His voice held a note of quiet gratitude, which echoed her own feelings.

Peyton clinked her mug against his. "To surviving," she agreed, taking a careful sip of the scalding liquid. It felt reassuringly mundane after the ordeal they'd just been through.

They sat in silence for a while, each lost in their own thoughts and savoring the comparative tranquility of the moment. The precinct around them hummed with activity as officers bustled about—cleaning up, preparing reports, dealing with the aftermath of Elliot Foster's reign of terror.

Outside, the sky blossomed into a bright blue canvas streaked with wisps of white clouds, as if the world was making an effort to heal itself just like them.

Peyton watched Sean from the corner of her eye. He looked tired but resilient, staring into his coffee as if seeking answers in its dark depths. The silence pooled and gathered, and it was an easy silence with no discomfort, the silence between old friends with no need to explain or pretend.

After a little while, Sean finished his coffee and set the mug aside. "I don't know about you," he said, "but I could sleep for about twenty hours. A hotel room is sounding mighty nice right about now."

"Tell me about it."

Peyton responded, letting her own mug join Sean's on the countertop. She felt the echoes of exhaustion roll over her again. It was surprising how a body could keep going when forced to its limits, but once safety was achieved, fragility seeped in with an almost overwhelming weight.

Sean rose to his feet with a slight wince before extending his hand to Peyton. "Come on," he said. "Let's get checked in."

She looked at his hand for a moment before placing her own into it, letting him pull her to her feet. They left the precinct in silence. Peyton felt like she was the one sleepwalking now, barely able to register a single detail around her.

As they got into the Jeep, Peyton tipped her seat back and closed her eyes. "You sure you'll be okay driving?" she asked.

"Should be," Sean responded with a light chuckle, sliding into the driver's seat. "If I start swerving, you have my permission to whack me awake."

Peyton cracked one eye open to glance at him skeptically. "Just don't start singing to keep yourself awake. Last time you did that, I was the one who wanted to jump out of the moving car."

Sean couldn't help but laugh at that memory, and the sound of it loosened something in Peyton. A sort of tension she hadn't known she was carrying unwound inside her chest. She grinned back at him, feeling the lines of fear and fatigue soften on her face.

"Deal," he said, his laughter subsiding to a smile. He turned the key in the ignition, and the car rumbled to life.

As they drove off from the precinct toward the hotel, Peyton thought about all they had faced. There was an odd sense of relief mingling with residual dread; the sensation of narrowly avoiding disaster was stark and real. But, for now, they were safe. They had survived, and that was all that mattered.

Sean drove in silence, with Peyton half-asleep beside him, her head against the window. The hum of the engine and the whoosh of tires over tarmac were oddly soothing.

Pulling up to the hotel, Sean nudged Peyton awake. "We're here," he murmured. Peyton blinked sleepily, straightening in her seat.

Together, they checked into the hotel and made their way up to their adjoining rooms. Peyton's room was simple and clean, a stark contrast to the chaotic swamp they'd just left behind. The soft hum of the air conditioner and the crisp white sheets on the bed beckoned her, promising rest she so desperately needed.

Sean wearily pushed his door open, glancing over his shoulder at Peyton. "See you in twenty hours?" he asked, an attempt at humor tugging at the corners of his mouth.

Peyton chuckled and nodded. "Twenty hours." She offered up a small salute, then turned to go inside her own room.

Once inside, she let out a huge sigh, sliding her bag off her tired shoulders and onto the floor. She could still feel the adrenaline simmering under her skin, but it was slowly being replaced by a sense of calm she hadn't felt in what seemed like forever.

As much as Peyton wanted to just drop into bed, she was all too aware of the swamp water still soaking her clothes.

Sighing, she forced herself to unpack a change of clothes from her bag, then made her way into the bathroom, peeling off the soaked layers as she went.

The hotel shower was a far cry from luxurious but the hot water pouring down on her felt like a balm to her tired body. It seemed to wash away not just the physical grime but also the mental strain of the past few hours. By the time she stepped out of the shower and into a soft hotel towel, Peyton felt somewhat human again.

Peyton padded back into the bedroom, pulling on clean clothes and letting her wet hair hang loose around her shoulders. As exhaustion continued to roll over her in waves, she moved toward the inviting bed.

Just before she climbed under the crisp sheets, she glanced out the window. The sky was now a brilliant shade of pink and gold as morning broke. For a moment, she drank in the beauty of it all.

Then, she was interrupted by a knock at the door.

She peered through the peephole and saw Sean standing there, shifting his weight uneasily from foot to foot.

"Sean?" Peyton asked, puzzled. "What's going on?"

Sean scratched his neck. "It's just..." He swallowed hard. Then, as if coming to a decision, he met her gaze. "Do you want to have dinner sometime? You know, like when you no longer feel like the 'swamp thing'?"

Peyton blinked, surprise cutting through her exhaustion for a moment. She was about to ask if he was joking, but the seriousness in his eyes told her he wasn't. Peyton let herself observe Sean, noting the fine lines of tiredness and resolve etched on his face. For more than a moment, she couldn't figure out what to say.

"Dinner?" she repeated, a little dumbfounded. But then she laughed, soft and low. It was such an absurd proposition given the context of their situation, yet an inexplicably warming one.

"Yeah," Sean said with a small shrug, a hint of vulnerability flickering across his eyes. "Like...a date." He scratched the back of his neck again, looking almost sheepish under her gaze. "I know it's probably the last thing on your mind right now, but I figured if I waited till tomorrow, I might chicken out. Better to strike while the adrenaline is still high, you know?"

Peyton chuckled lightly at his words, crossing her arms over her chest as she leaned against the doorway. The strange mix of exhaustion and exhilaration she was feeling seemed to swirl together into a white-hot bubble of laughter in her chest. "A date, huh?"

Sean nodded, shuffling his feet a little. His eyes were steady on hers, though, shining with a thread of hope. "What do you say?"

A mirthful smile spread across her face then, softening her careworn features under the warm glow of the hallway lights. The absurdity of it all was almost endearing in its own way. Finally, with a shrug and a light chuckle, she said, "Sure, Sean. A date it is."

Sean's face immediately brightened, the tired lines around his eyes smoothing out for the first time since they'd left the precinct. His shoulders relaxed as he exhaled in relief, his lightheartedness returning as a teasing grin lit his face. "And here I was, ready to beg."

Peyton rolled her eyes but couldn't hide the smile playing at the corners of her mouth. "Save your begging for dinner, Sean. You're going to need it if you end up ordering that disgusting seafood dish you like so much."

Sean held a hand to his heart, feigning hurt. "I'll have you know, Peyton," he said with mock sternness, "that calamari is a delight of the sea and a testament to mankind's culinary genius."

Peyton gave a small laugh, shaking her head at him. Despite the mirthful exchange, she could see in his eyes the sincerity of his request. He was offering more than dinner; he was offering a momentary reprieve from their reality—a chance for them to be just Sean and Peyton without the weight of their job bearing down on them.

And that, she believed, was the very antidote she needed for everything she'd just been through.

"Good night, Sean," she said with a faint smile, her eyes flicking up to meet his one last time before she closed the door.

Alone once more, Peyton leaned back against the door. Her heart was pounding, but for the first time in a while, it was pounding with excitement, not fear.

EPILOGUE

Peyton stirred her puttanesca, not really hungry any more, her mind on the video she'd been looking at just a few days ago at Mountain View Storage. She recalled the way Sean had shown up out of the blue to tell her about their latest case and how she'd immediately closed the laptop and then acted as if nothing was on her mind.

I lied to him, she thought, feeling suddenly guilty. Then again, her investigation into her parents' mysterious deaths was an intensely personal matter, and she hadn't felt ready to share her findings with Sean.

Didn't she have the right to decide what she shared, and when?

Yes, you do. But that doesn't mean you had to lie to him.

The restaurant was buzzing with life as waiters moved in swift choreography, balancing plates and trays, weaving around customers. The clinking of glasses and the soft murmur of conversation provided a backdrop to her wandering thoughts. The chandeliers hung low, casting soft dancing shadows over the tables.

Peyton sank back in her chair, her thoughts a swirling, chaotic cloud.

"Something on your mind?" Sean asked. He was spearing a piece of calamari with his fork and seeming to take immense pleasure in it.

Peyton smiled slightly, pushing the pasta around her plate. "Just thinking," she said. It wasn't the entire truth, but it wasn't a lie, either.

Back at Mountain View Storage, Sean hadn't pressed for answers. Now, however, he leaned back in his chair, wiped his mouth with a cloth napkin, and cocked his head curiously at her.

"Of course you're thinking," he said. "Care to share the subject of your ruminations?"

Tell him, she thought. *He deserves to know after everything you two have been through.*

She looked at Sean. He was waiting for her, and she had the sense that he would wait a long time for her to speak—all night, perhaps. She felt undeserving, thinking of how she'd deceived him.

She set her fork down. "Want to go for a walk?"

Sean quirked an eyebrow. "I thought you wanted dessert. They have the best tiramisu in town," he said, a playful smile tugging at the corners of his lips.

Peyton shook her head, her eyes meeting his with a mixture of determination and vulnerability. "Not tonight, Sean. I need to talk to you about something important."

The smile faded from Sean's face, replaced by a look of concern. He nodded, placing his napkin on the table and standing up. "Of course, Peyton. Let's take that walk."

Sean signaled to the waiter, who brought the check. Sean pulled out a credit card.

"Really, you don't have to," Peyton began, but Sean waved a hand.

"Don't worry about it," he said. "My treat."

Afterward, they rose and headed outside. They were still in Louisiana – they each had the next few days off, and they had both expressed a desire to do some sightseeing, since their investigation hadn't really afforded them the opportunity to enjoy their time here – and the night was warm, the air thick with the scent of the bayou. Crickets chirped rhythmically in the distance, and the sky was a canvas of stars, unhindered by city lights.

Sean led the way down a cobblestone street lined with charming houses cocooned in climbing ivy and blooming hydrangeas. Their shoes clicked softly against the stones as their silence filled the space between them. Peyton felt a small knot of anxiety in her stomach. She wondered how he would react to her confession.

They were nearing a park by the time she finally gathered her courage. "Back at Mountain View Storage..." she started, her voice hitching slightly before she cleared her throat. "I found something...something about my parents' murder."

Sean stopped in his tracks, surprise registering on his face. A thousand questions swarmed over his face, but he remained silent, waiting.

"I found a video on a thumb drive," she said. "On the video..." She paused, then sighed and pulled out her phone. "I guess I'd better show it to you."

Sean's gaze followed Peyton as she scrolled through her phone, her brows drawn together in concentration. There was a palpable tension in the air, broken only by the occasional rustle of the trees surrounding them.

Peyton played the video and handed her phone to Sean. He watched it in silence, his face impassive. Peyton listened to the audio, having seen the video often enough to picture exactly what was happening.

"—and I thought you and I had an understanding," a man with a nasal voice said. "But apparently I was wrong."

"I'm sure we can figure this out," Galen, Peyton's father, said. *Ever the diplomat,* Peyton thought sadly. Some people, however, couldn't be appeased.

"I sure hope so," the stranger said. "But just in case, I brought along a little...insurance."

There was a pause in the sound—this, Peyton knew, was where the stranger was showing her father a picture of Peyton at school when she was twelve. In the picture, she was smiling into the camera, her hair in messy braids, completely unaware of the danger that was about to befall her parents.

"Don't you dare hurt my daughter," Galen said with barely-controlled anger. There was fear wrapped up in that anger, too.

"Then don't make me," the man said, sounding almost casual. "It's all in your hands. You do what I want, or else..."

Sean's gaze was fixed on the screen, his jaw tightening as the video ended. For several moments, he continued to stare at the screen. Then he glanced up at Peyton and shook his head, looking awfully angry himself.

"Who is he?" he asked. "Who's the bastard who threatened you?"

"I don't know," Peyton said helplessly. "I don't recognize him."

Sean was silent for a moment, staring back at the screen as if it held more answers. "You're sure?" he asked, his voice low.

Peyton nodded, her throat constricted. "I've played it over and over, Sean," she admitted. "I was hoping I'd recognize something, anything... But there's nothing. All I know is that my dad must've known something was seriously wrong for him to be secretly recording their conversation. But what did he get mixed up in?"

Sean's hand clenched around her phone as he handed it back to her. The silence that followed was almost deafening, only punctuated by the distant chirping of crickets and the hushed rustling of leaves.

He looked out into the myriad of shadows cast by the trees. "Why didn't you tell me sooner, Peyton?"

She bit her lip, wringing her hands as she looked at him. "I...I don't know," she admitted. She felt a sting of tears behind her eyes, but she blinked them away. "I was scared, I guess."

A moment of silence passed between them before Sean finally broke it, turning back to look at her. "I understand," he said quietly. "It

141

must have been difficult for you to carry this alone. But Peyton," he moved closer, his gaze soft with concern, "you're not alone in this anymore."

His words felt like a balm on an old wound. She felt some of the tension dissipate from her shoulders, and she let out a small sigh. "Thank you, Sean," she said, her voice barely more than a whisper.

Sean nodded wordlessly, grabbing her hand and giving it a reassuring squeeze. They continued their walk in silence, meandering through the park in no particular direction, the weight of what they just shared suspended between them.

As they neared an ornate bench beneath a weeping willow tree, Peyton felt Sean's steps slow. He guided her to the bench, and they sat down, the darkness of the night offering a comforting blanket. Patches of light trickled through the leaves from an old streetlamp nearby.

"Peyton," Sean said, his voice soft and earnest. "We're going to figure this out. We'll find out who this man is and what he wanted from your father."

Peyton gave him a small nod, looking at the man beside her. His face was stern, focused, and she knew in that moment that Sean was a man of his word. He would help her. If she had any doubt about telling him before, it was all erased now.

"But we need to tread carefully," he continued, his gaze never leaving hers. "Whoever this man is...he's dangerous."

"I understand," Peyton replied quietly, her heart pounding with a mix of fear and determination. She knew what they were up against wouldn't be easy or safe, but she also couldn't stand the idea of leaving her parents' murderers unpunished.

"I think he may have killed my parents," Peyton said in a choked whisper.

Sean was silent for a moment, his gaze holding hers in the dim light. He squeezed her hand, his touch a warm and solid presence against her turmoil. "We don't know that yet," he finally said. "But we'll find out. We're going to uncover every rock, every possibility, until we do."

Peyton nodded, drawing in a shaky breath as she fought to steady herself. She felt Sean's thumb gently brushing over her knuckles in an attempt to soothe her, the gesture making her feel less alone.

"I know," Peyton said after a long pause. She stared at their entwined hands and then back at him with a newfound resolve in her eyes. "And when we do...if we find out he's responsible..." She swallowed hard. "I'm going to get justice for my parents. No matter what."

NOW AVAILABLE!

WHAT'S MINE
(A Peyton Risk Suspense Thriller—Book Five)

In the harsh glare of the desert, a mastermind killer leaves victims to die of exposure in the wilderness, leaving behind chilling clues, drawings on canyon walls. National Parks Officer Peyton Risk, an expert at solving homicides within the National parks, has seen it all, and is summoned to hunt him down. With Peyton's deep knowledge of the wilderness, she knows the parks as no one else does. Yet this killer seems to operate by no rules whatsoever....

WHAT'S MINE (A Peyton Risk Suspense Thriller—Book 5) is Book #5 in a new series by mystery and suspense author Ella Swift.

Raised in the heart of the mountains by avid outdoors enthusiasts, Peyton followed in her parents' footsteps and became an expert in the natural world. Until, at just 12 years old, an idyllic family camping trip in their favorite national park turned into a nightmare. Her parents were brutally murdered, the killer vanished into the wild, and the case went cold.

Despite being haunted by the unsolved deaths of her parents, Peyton turned her trauma into determination, studying environmental science in college and becoming a respected National Parks Officer. Peyton's unique perspective blends an intuition for the outdoors with a sharp intellect that allows her to decipher secrets hidden within the parks— set on ensuring that no other family endures the same pain that hers did.

But will she find herself the next victim claimed in the park's unforgiving wilderness?

A page-turning and harrowing thriller featuring a brilliant and tortured protagonist, the PEYTON RISK series is a riveting mystery, packed with non-stop action, suspense, twists and turns, revelations, and driven by a breakneck pace that will keep you flipping pages late into the night.

Future books in the series are also available!

Ella Swift

Ella Swift is author of the PEYTON RISK mystery series, comprising five books (and counting).

An avid reader and lifelong fan of the mystery and thriller genres, Ella loves to hear from you, so please feel free to visit ellaswiftauthor.com to learn more and stay in touch.

BOOKS BY ELLA SWIFT

PEYTON RISK MYSTERY SERIES
WHAT'S HIS (Book #1)
WHAT'S LEFT (Book #2)
WHAT'S WISHED (Book #3)
WHAT'S GONE (Book #4)
WHAT'S MINE (Book #5)

Made in the USA
Las Vegas, NV
25 March 2025

20115831R00090